MAGIC
WONDERLAND

MAGIC WONDERLAND

SANDA BOCA

MAGIC WONDERLAND

This is a work of fiction. All of the characters, names, incidents,
organizations, and dialogue in this novel are either the products
of the author's imagination or are used fictitiously.

iUniverse books may be ordered through booksellers or by contacting:

iUniverse
1663 Liberty Drive
Bloomington, IN 47403
www.iuniverse.com
844-349-9409

Edited by: Sally Sak

Because of the dynamic nature of the Internet, any web addresses or
links contained in this book may have changed since publication and
may no longer be valid. The views expressed in this work are solely those
of the author and do not necessarily reflect the views of the publisher,
and the publisher hereby disclaims any responsibility for them.

Any people depicted in stock imagery provided by Getty Images are
models, and such images are being used for illustrative purposes only.
Certain stock imagery © Getty Images.

ISBN: 978-1-6632-4685-1 (sc)
ISBN: 978-1-6632-4684-4 (e)

Library of Congress Control Number: 2022919051

Print information available on the last page.

iUniverse rev. date: 12/01/2022

BEGINNING OF JOURNEY

It is a beautiful Saturday morning in September. The sun is up with no clouds in the sky.

Victor is sleeping quietly in his little bed. Today is his birthday. Multiple coloured balloons and gifts wrapped in bright coloured paper fill his room. Beside his bed there is a small desk with his books on it. A tall lamp is close to the door and gives a pale light to the room.

The sun rays touched his eyes and his forehead gently until he opened his eyes, and he remembered what his mom told him the night before:

> "Tomorrow, my darling, you will be 10 years old. We will go to a magical place called "Magic Wonderland", where your imagination will become reality, your dreams will come true and you will see, there are many more surprises in that world."

> "Can I take Khalifa with me?" Victor asked.

Khalifa is his fluffy black cat, with long hair and round green eyes. When Khalifa heard his name, he looked at Victor's mom with big, opened his eyes and put his ears up like two antennas. He wanted to hear everything.

> "Of course, his mom said, brushing his hair gently with her fingers. Khalifa will always be by your side. He will play with you; talk with you, and…"

"Talk with me?" Victor interrupted his mom.

He wanted to believe. In fact, he does because he is sure that he heard his cat talking to him from time to time; little words only, but still…he spoke. But how can somebody believe this? Even at his age he knew that this could not be possible.

> "And he will grant all your wishes. This is the place of all possibilities. It is where my parents took me and my sister when we were your age and we never wanted to go anywhere else. This is where I spent all my vacations and even that was not enough. But there is one trick: you must believe, my son. If you believe, you will see, and if you see, you will believe. The faith opens a gate to the unknown where magic becomes reality, and the reality feels like magic. And this is magical!" said Sanda, his mom, with a nostalgia in her voice.

Victor knew that he fell asleep thinking about all the mysteries promised for his birthday. He wondered how it will be and could hardly wait to talk with his little cat. Having a talking cat is something, but what else is there to believe?

Now he is awake and remembers everything. He jumped out of his bed and ran to his mom's room.

"Mom, mom, wake up!!"

Khalifa was right there beside Victor, looking in his eyes with big round green cute eyes.

"We will go to the magic place!" Victor said. He jumped in her bed. "Daddy is coming too, right?"

His mom opened her eyes, and gave her son a big hug, kissed his forehead and his round rosy cheeks.

"Yes, dear. Daddy will come soon. He wouldn't miss your birthday for anything in the world. Let's get ready now. I was waiting so long for this day."

In that moment the entrance door opened, and Victor could hear his daddy's voice:

"Happy Birthday my dear son! May your days be filled with magic, innocence to guide you, and may your heart be always pure so you will always see and believe. Happy birthday, my dear son!

His father, Alex, stepped into the bedroom with a big birthday cake. On its top, there were ten lighted candles.

"Daddy, daddy!!" Victor screamed happily and jumped out of bed. He ran to his father. His father took him in his arms. He kissed his forehead and then said:

"Happy birthday, my son. I wish for you to enjoy your life to the fullest, and never lose your faith in magic. The magic will fill your life with so much wonder and every single day you will want more of it. Now, make a wish and blow the candles."

"I wish... "Victor said

"No, honey, do not tell us your wish. If you say it out laud it will not come true. The wish is just for you, and the universe will grant it. Now make a wish in your mind and when you are ready, blow the candles." Victor's mom said.

Victor closed his round brown eyes, made a wish in his mind, looked at his parents and blew the candles.

They all started to laugh when the candles were out. His mom said:

"Who wants cake?"

"Me, me" said Victor and his father.

They all went to the dining room. The table was already prepared for a celebration. Three white plates and silverware were on the round table, along with a small vase full of fresh red roses in the middle. Their scent engulfed the air in the whole room.

Victor, curious about his magical birthday surprise asked his parents:

"Is it far? What will happen to the Magic Wonderland? When will Khalifa talk with me?"

"Be patient" his father said. "Everything will be revealed today just for you."

Victor was the first one to finish his slice of cake. He asked politely if he can be dismissed and when his wish was granted, he went in his bedroom and started to dress up. Victor took a pair of short blue pants, a white T-shirt, and blue shoes. He loved them. His mom took him shopping and he chose his outfit for this day.

IS THIS REAL OR MAGIC?

It was a short walking distance to the Magic Wonderland. When they got in front of the entrance, there were many children with their parents around them. Some kids had popcorn in their hands; some had ice cream, some balloons, and some had their faces hidden in cotton candy.

"Look at the right door, my son, there's the entrance" Sanda, Victor's mom, said.

Victor looked at the right and there was a big crystal door with a white swan, and a white rabbit dressed like a doorman in front of it. Through the crystal door, he could see many children laughing and playing. A big sign in bright colourful lights was on top of the door which says: MAGIC WONDERLAND. Fireworks kept flashing all around the sign. Victor and Khalifa's eyes were sparkling in the lights. His mom's heart was filled with so much love for her little angel. She knew deep in her heart that her son believed and seen.

On the swan's head, there was a gold crown with many rubies all around and the tips of the feathers had rubies as well. On his legs, he had gold rings with red sparkling rubies.

A little funny white mouse was beating a little drum. Victor heard the swan talking out loud:

> "Hello, hello, my dear children. My name is Thiassi. I am the King of the Birds' Realm. I am honoured today to welcome you all inside this magic world" he said, and he bowed gently. "Here you can have free ice cream, free candies, as many hotdogs as you want, free rides, magical animals to play with, and you can have as many wishes as you want. Everything you want! If you are naughty, your wishes will be granted in a naughty way. If you are good, your wishes will come true. Be aware what you wish for, my dear friends. Bring in your darling parents. But remember, only those pure of heart can believe and see this gate. If you do not believe, you do not see, and you can't come inside."

Victor looked around and has seen many children that heard the swan and wanted to go there. They asked their parents to go to the Magic Wonderland. Some parents didn't believe and didn't see the crystal door. The parents tried to explain to their children that they are going to Wonderland, but the door is to the left. Victor felt sad to see some children disappointed.

He wondered why the people didn't hear the swan and he asked his mom. She told him:

> "My son, it takes courage to keep a pure heart all your life. The heart must remain innocent to understand the world that is unfolded under our eyes and to live it."

Khalifa remembered when he was here and played with Victor's mom and her sister, when they were little girls. While impatiently waiting to go inside, he said to Victor:

> "Victor let's go and play. Today is your birthday and I will make sure all your wishes will come true!"

Victor looked at his cat, then at his mom, and asked:

> "Mom! Did you hear him?! Khalifa is talking!!!"

> "Yes, my dear. I heard him. He is talking with you. He always did, and you heard him sometimes. From now on, you will hear him all the time. Now, let's go inside and let the wonderful journey begin!"

Nemo, the doorman rabbit, looked at Victor, his parents and Khalifa. He touched his chin with his soft paws as he wondered which star to give to them.

There are four different coloured stars. Each color of the star is the key to enter in the same colour realm. Blue is for children that want the power to control the water and to play with it, Green for children who can see and talk with all the animals and birds, and Red is for the children who love magic. And then there is Gold. Gold is only for a special child who wants to explore and wants to know everything; it is for a child that his thirst for knowledge of reality and magic has no limits.

"Hmm, Nemo continued. This is a hard choice. Hmm... yes, yes. We have a special one here. I haven't seen a special one for a long time. There was once a girl that used to come here all the time with her sister. Their names were Sanda and Gabriela. They always got a gold star. Their hearts were pure, open, and their voices were soft. Their imagination for new and magical world was envied by the most known wizards and witches. I wonder where they are now."

"Here I am, my dear Nemo, said Victor's mom. I am standing right in front of you with my son Victor, his father Alex, and our cat Khalifa. I am sure you remember Khalifa. We missed you so much! About my sister, Gabriela, I hope she will be here today."

"I didn't see her just yet, my dear Sanda. I am sure she will not miss today and tomorrow. Tomorrow is her little son's birthday if I remember correctly. Please excuse an old rabbit for his memory; sometimes it plays tricks on me. But, hey! Yay! I hardly can wait to give them gold stars. For sure her children are like her, with the undeniable thirst for knowledge. I miss her" said Nemo with nostalgia in his voice. "I missed you too, my dear Sanda. Good memories. Right, Mr. Khalifa?"

Khalifa went in front of the rabbit, bowed, and said:

> "I am honoured to see you again, Mr. Nemo. Good memories enlightened my life and now I am extremely delighted that I can pass them onto Victor. Today he reaches the age of most curiosity and thirst for knowledge."

> "Hello Mr. Khalifa" the rabbit said. "I am so honoured to see again the King of Small Animals' Realm. You are a true leader, my dear friend. You always have been."

> "I am thinking to pass the crown to another small animal from our realm, now that all my time will be much occupied with teaching and guiding Victor into the reality of the unseen and unknown world. But this is just a thought for now. You never know what the end of the day will bring. I have big plans to make all his wishes come true. It is so good to see you again. Now please give us the star so we can go inside and begin our journey into the unknown!"

> "With pleasure, my dear friend. GOLD! GOLD STAR HERE!" said Nemo out loud as he bowed to them while they passed through the gate.

A bright and shiny gold star appeared on the back of Victor's right hand.

Victor looked at it with wonder. He tried to erase it with the other hand, but the star became brighter and brighter.

"Mom, dad, look at my star! It is so beautiful! I can't erase it! The colour is stronger! Wow… It's amazing!"

Everyone around stopped talking and looked at them. They all knew what it means to get a gold star. They knew that someone special is there and all children wanted to go to play with Victor, but they were limited by their coloured stars. They were not allowed to go and play in other places, only in the ones selected by their star which were their wishes. They knew that they must wait in their realm for Victor to go there and then they can play with him.

Victor was very happy to get a gold star, but he didn't understand why other children cannot go everywhere in the Wonderland to see everything, it was a Magic Wonderland after all. But he didn't pay too much attention to this detail. He knew that he would meet them all and will make many friends today.

"Where do you want to go first? To play with the water, play with the dragons and lions or play with magic?" Khalifa asked.

"I want to see and play with them all! Do the animals like sweets? Can we get some ice cream, candies, and cakes to share with them?

Victor stopped talking and he realized something sensational. He continued:

"Khalifa, you are talking with me, and I understand you!! How is this possible?" Victor asked.

"My dearest friend, I always talked to you. You just didn't believe that there is magic in your world. Don't feel bad, nobody does...ha-ha-ha." Khalifa said. "And about our animal friends, yes, they love the ice cream and candies and cakes and all human foods. There is never enough for them.... Ha-ha-ha! Let's share."

Somewhere, in the realm, under a crystal dome, a hyena just woke up from a thousand-year spell.

"Khalifa? Did I hear right?" Shadow said to himself. *"It is time to take my revenge. Hi-hi-hi, he will pay today. I have been waiting for far too long."*

Shadow is a naughty hyena who believes that everything belongs to him. Well, this is what his mother told him when he was a puppy, and he came to truly believed it. He just woke up and while stretching his bones, he was yawning too laud.

Did anybody hear him?

It is quite questionable; he was covered by an invisible crystal shield.

"Oh, I had such a good nap. I feel so rested" Shadow was thinking out loud. *"Khalifa, you will pay today! Do you hear me? I can't forgive you for what you have done to me!"* Shadow screamed.

"I will find a way to show you that I am the best. I should be the King of Small Animals Realm, not you. You are too weak. Just wait and see. I am coming for you!" Shadow continued, being very frustrated that nobody can hear him.

GREEN REALM

Just thinking about ice cream, an old ice cream carriage appeared in front of them. There was Mr. Ali, the Turkish man who comes on their street every day to give ice cream, cakes, and candies to all children. He is very popular in the area. He makes the best ice cream, and everybody waits for him to come on the street. He is always laughing when offering different flavours of ice cream cones.

By now he knows everyone's favorites and when he sees them, he calls them with his strong Turkish accent:

"Take ice cream from Ali. The best for you. Ha, ha, ha. I have them all! Chocolate, strawberry, vanilla, rose, maple, lemon, and fire ice cream."

"Oh, I see Sanda here! I heard she came with her son Victor, and he got a gold star. Of course, the apple doesn't fall far from the tree. Ha, ha, ha...I knew it...Where is Gabriela? That sweet little girl loves my lemon ice cream the most."

"Hmmm...she will be here today. I must look for her" was thinking Mr. Ali.

"What is fire ice cream?" Victor wondered. *"It must be something new!"*

"Good morning, Mr. Ali. Please give us many fire ice cream cones, four cakes and two handfuls of candies! We want to visit the animals to offer some to them" Victor said.

"Good choice, Victor. Right, Mr. Khalifa?" Mr. Ali asked.

"Right, my friend. It always fills my tummy, ha, ha, ha. And I can have as much as I want from the same cone." Khalifa said.

The fire ice cream has a special flavour; it tastes like nothing else in the whole world. Only Mr. Ali knows the recipe and it is his secret. There is fire in a cone, and it burns with white and gold flames. When you want to eat some, the flames are cold. You can eat as much as you want, and the cone will always be full. The flames fill up the cones again and again.

Mr. Ali filled up a tray with the fire ice cream cones, cakes, and candies. Sanda took them and gave one to Victor and one to Khalifa.

"I missed the ice cream here. I had it last week on our street, but it tastes soooo muuuuch betttter here.... wow!... I love it!" said Khalifa. "Victor, do you know why this ice cream is so special? Not only does it have a unique taste, but it gives you the power to sense what animals, birds, and nature feel. It connects you with

15

them all. You are one with everything that surrounds you. Do you understand what I am saying?"

"Everything you say" Victor answered with his mouth full of ice cream. "I just need you to show me everything, please. I do not know how to connect with the birds, animals, and nature."

"Sure!" Khalifa said excitedly. "It is my pleasure and my duty! Every time you wish for something in your mind, the birds, animals, and the nature hear you. They all rush to fulfill your wish. You will feel their kindness and endless love for everybody. Now I would like to have some candies, while you make friends in this part of Wonderland. It is full of wonders. And do not forget, all your wishes will come true everywhere in this magical land. What is your first wish for today? You can ask for anything and I will grant them all to you."

"I want to play with all children. I want them all to be my friends."

"Great wish, my friend. Now close your eyes and when you are ready just open them up and all the children in this part of the Wonderland will be here with you."

Victor closed his eyes and in seconds, he said:

"I am ready now!" and he opened his eyes.

A whole new world opened up before his eyes. The children were riding dragons, unicorns, huge birds, and many other mythical creatures that he never heard of or seen before. Other children were sliding down the long necks of dinosaurs, roaring of laughter. Many roller coasters were filled with children's laughs; children playing in the pools, and others just walking proudly with their animal friends. Green fields and beautiful flowers were all around, while mountains were seen in the far distance.

"Hello everybody! My name is Victor. We have fire ice cream, candies, and cakes for all of you. Please come and have some."

Victor was amazed as he looked around. His parents, the children and even the magical creatures who heard him, all came up to him.

"I want to play with the animals!" he told Khalifa.

"Just think about which one you want, and it will be here" Khalifa answered.

"I want a lion. They are big and scary" Victor replied.

"Not in this part of the world, my dear friend. All animals here are friendly and willing to follow your command. I can become anything you want me to be, "said Khalifa.

"Can you be a big, big lion?"

"I am so happy you asked. I will be the Dragan Lion" Khalifa said very proud.

"What's a Dragan Lion?" Victor asked confused.

"My friend, I am a gigantic lion born way before the Moon lit up the sky in the night. I had golden skin which was impenetrable to the weapons, and my claws were sharper than any sword or arrow used by mortals, or humans as you would call them.

Many centuries ago, people were talking about the strongest man in the world who was asked to kill the giant lion, not me to be precise - I am still here! The lion, named Typhon has been terrorizing Dragan Valley, a small village in Transylvania's Mountain. He was searching for the lion and when he finally found it, the strong man shot arrows at him, but he knew he couldn't kill the giant lion. This was just the show he put on for the villagers who were watching. The lion was very wise, and magic was his way of doing things. You see, people at that time didn't know anything about us. But they were smart and always found for clever ways of discovering the unknown. Bogdan, the bravest and stronger man found a way to trap the giant lion. He put carrots and potatoes in his barn, closed one of the entrances, and was waiting for my brother. When Typhon entered the barn, the strongest and wisest man closed the door behind them. Nobody knew that he could talk with animals. Typhon felt trapped inside.

"Do not be afraid," Bogdan said to Typhon. "I am not here to harm you."

"Really? What about the arrows you shot at me?" Typhon asked.

"I knew they cannot harm you. It was for the villagers to see that I follow their command" said Bogdan with a kind voice.

"What do you want?" asked my brother.

"I need to know why you are here, in this small village. That's all." Bogdan said.

"I am looking for food, for myself and my younger brother. That's all" Typhon said.

"So…you don't want to eat anyone?"

"Ha-ha-ha…that's funny. We eat carrots and potatoes, and sometimes, if we are lucky, we eat corn" said Typhon laughing out loud.

"Do you know that the villagers asked me to kill you? I don't want to do that. Can we go somewhere where you will not be harmed?" asked Bogdan.

Typhon was looking at Khalifa, who was right beside him, and he knew the right answer in an instant.

———————⟫⟪———————

Khalifa entered the barn before his brother, but Bogdan didn't see him. He was distracted by his dog who was barking loudly.

"Please, stop barking" Bogdan asked Alun, his dog. "The villagers will hear and will come here. We don't want that, do we?"

"No, we don't. I don't like them." Alun said. "I don't want you to kill anybody, especially this majestic lion. I like him."

"I like him too." said Bogdan to his dog.

———— ◦◦◦◦ ————

"Come with us in a world where we will live forever, and you will be my best friend,"

Typhon exclaimed with joy. "What do you say?"

"Can I bring Alun with me? He is my very devoted dog and I love him very much."

"Sure, he will be my friend too." said Typhon." Khalifa, please lead the way."

They all came to this magical wonderland.

"Where is your brother now?" Victor asked.

"He is right there in the mountains with Bogdan and Alun. They spend all the time together having the time of their life." said Khalifa.

"You mentioned the time before the Moon lit up the sky in the night. When was that?" Victor asked.

"At the beginning of time, the Moon was born in a far universe. Her mother, The Mother Iron Planet, was dying. She knew that her inner light was fading fast, and she took her Moon, as she called her child, on a long journey throughout the universe to find a home for her baby planet. They travelled tremendous distances until they found Earth. The Moon felt like home right here. She fell in love with the green grass, the blue oceans, and people of the Earth, and she loved the warmth of the sun on her face. She wished to have the power to lit up the Earth during the night. Her wish was granted, and she is circling the Earth to this day. She sees everything: day and night. She is happy here. Her home is here. She didn't want to leave. Her mother, feeling happy that her baby is safe here, continued her journey to the Infinite Knowledge, where she will rest for eternity," said Khalifa.

"What do you mean by "she didn't want to leave"?" asked Victor.

"There were countless moons to come and thought they found a place to stay here forever. Only they didn't love our planet, and they didn't want to light the sky in the night. They were dark, small planets. Mother Earth knew that and sent them all away until Moon came. Mother Earth loved Moon's kindness, and there will always be a connection between them. They are happy, this all that counts." continued Khalifa.

"Wow. I didn't know that." said Victor. "Khalifa, do you know if there is a meaning of the name Bogdan?"

"It means the "Gift of God"." answered Khalifa.

A big tornado of bright colours started to cover Khalifa, going up, and eventually reaching the blue sky. Thunder, lights, and rainbows surrounded his body. Khalifa grew into a giant magnificent lion with golden skin. A roar coming from his big chest froze the noise all around them. Complete silence followed. Children looked at Victor, and they knew he is the chosen one.

"Come and play with us!" a friendly girl said. "I am Tannis, and this is my little sister Brittany."

They were both riding a dragon with big golden eyes, a gold body, and red wings. Her tail was shooting rays of red. She looked magnificent.

"Her name is SunSinger. She likes to sing on sunny days, and her voice is so beautiful. We can even change the colour of our dragon!" Tannis said. "Do you want to see?"

"Yes, please!" Victor said. "How do you do it?"

"Just think about it and they will know. All animals here can read our minds."

Tannis closed her eyes and, in her mind gave a command to her dragon.

The dragon became ivory blue with light blue eyes. Her body and wings were so big that the two sisters looked like little dolls on her back. The dragon said in a soft voice:

"I can be a dragon, or a wolf, or a penguin, whatever the children want. All animals can do that in this part of the world. Their wish is our command."

"Wow! Mom, Dad, it's amazing. Did you see that?!" Victor said.

"Yes, my dear, we saw, and we are so happy that you have discovered the meaning and the power of magic. We can control everything with our minds in this Magic Wonderland. When our minds are strong, and hearts are open and innocent, magical things will happen. Just let them happen, my dear son" Victor's mother said.

"Thank you, mom, I will. Khalifa, you are a lion, but can you fly?"

"Jump on my back."

Big wings appeared in an instant on Khalifa's back, and then he pushed his front legs hard against the ground and was ready to take off.

"Where do you want to go?" Khalifa asked Victor.

"Everywhere! I want to see everything!"

"Hold on to my hair and enjoy the ride, my dear friend."

"Let's give first fire ice cream to the kids and to the animals. But we do not have enough for everybody" Victor said with sadness in his voice.

"Do not worry, my friend. The more you give, the more there will be to give."

"Okay. Wahoo!!" Victor shouted with excitement.

Victor shared the fire ice cream with the children and their mythical animals around. The more he gave, the more sweets filled his trays.

Then, he jumped on Khalifa's back and they both flew up into the sky. There were children flying dragons, Yales, Roc birds, Firebirds, Griffins, Unicorns, and many more mythical animals. It was a different world.

"I am Victor, and this is my cat, Khalifa. Now he is a winged lion. He is my best friend" Victor said to a boy with red hair.

"I am Doodley, and this is my little mouse. Her name is Julie. She is my devoted dragon in this wonderland. I love her long neck, and I can slide on it as if I were on a toboggan…yay!! And by the way, I am from New York, the city of opportunities, as my mother says" Doodley added with pride in his voice.

"Hi. I am Amber and this is my Unicorn. Her name is Celestia, which means "from the stars". She is my puppy and very naughty in our real world; she likes to hide and chew my shoes. Celestia likes it here very much and she can also read my mind! I was born in Iceland and when I was five, my father got a job in Tennessee, so we have lived there ever since."

"Hello. I am Aden. I came from Gold City, a holy place in Tibet. My parents brought me here just to visit this magic wonderland. People in Tibet are talking about this place, but nobody has ever been here before. My parents love adventures, and they say this is the best adventure we will have in our life. Look at them. They are flying on that white giant eagle's wings, yelling "Wahoo!". I can't wait to go back to tell everybody about this place!"

"Hmm…this ice cream is so gooood…. By the way this is my Yale, Cory. His teeth are big and sharp, but he is very gentle. He shows them only when he laughs, and he laughs a lot. I had him as a puppy wolf, and I raised him as my dog. As you can see, a yale has a head and body of a goat, tail and tusks of a boar, and the feet of a unicorn. "Aden said.

Cory started to laugh so hard, that Aden almost fell from his back.

"Why are you laughing now, Cory? What's so funny?"

"This fire ice cream makes me happy. I just remembered when I was a puppy and my mother, the Yale Queen, used to bring me here. She taught me how to become the lovely friend I am now…ha-ha-ha. I was trained by the best of the best! My mom trained many animals. For the ones that were not here at that time, she left the knowledge within the air of this realm. Therefore, all animals that come here for the first time know everything in an instant. It's in the air for everybody; animals and children alike."

"Even for us?" Aden asked.

"How else can you explain that here all children can talk with all animals, or by just thinking about them make them appear wishing to make the children's dreams come true? Why do I have wings and I can fly? Because you wished for it. Ask Mr. Khalifa, he was here for a long time. I believe he was here from the beginning of life when magic and reality were one. There was no difference between them at that time."

"It is true, my honorable friend Cory" Khalifa responded. "Countless generations enjoyed this part of the world. I lost count of how many generations came here since the beginning of time. We tried to keep it the same, and it was not hard at all. All animals are pure at heart and made this world to be real."

"Hello, my name is Tony. I am from Verona, the City of Love in Italy, as my father told me. My father knew this magic place from his father, and his father from my grandpa, and so on, for eight generations. They all loved to come here. I will pass on this knowledge to my children and my grandchildren. Until then, my farm of parrots will be with me" Tony continued as he showed his parrots off to all children. "I wanted them to be parrots here also, they are my best friends. I didn't want to change them. I love them all so much."

Children and parents were looking at Tony with admiration. He was sitting in a hammock made of parrots' feathers and hundreds of colourful parrots were holding it.

"This is Willy, Benny, Berny, Tory, Louis, Coco, Harley, Smokey, Pepper, Ruby, Robby, Falcon,

Mystique, Miss Lady, Murphy, Jessy, Barry, Mario, Toby, Nimbus and …all their babies! Say "Hello" to everybody" he said to the birds.

"Hello, hello!" the little birds said. They imitated Tony's voice so clearly, that you could swear it was Tony speaking.

"Trained them well, didn't I?" Tony said with pride in his voice. "The beauty is that I can play with them all day long, after school of course."

"Victor, Victor, Victor!!"

Three voices were heard from the distance, coming closer and closer.

Victor looked in that direction and saw the biggest bird with three boys, like three little dots flying on her back. It was the gigantic Roc bird. The bird had red feathers with yellow and orange feathers on her wings. In the sun light, the wings were shiny like they were on fire.

Shadow was watching Khalifa and Victor from inside the dome. He wished he could exit the dome and harm them, but he couldn't, not just yet. He had to be patient a little bit longer. He wanted revenge. He wanted to be the King of Small Animal's Realm. He was born to be a King, his mother told him that many times.

While he was thinking which the best way is to hurt Khalifa, he saw the big bird with three kids on her back coming to Victor.

> *"What now? Who are they?"* Shadow was wondering. *"I need to find Victor alone, kidnap him, and Khalifa will give me the crown in exchange for Victor"* Shadow was thinking. *"Hi-hi-hi, this is a good plan. Now is my time!"*

FAMILY REUNITED

"Victor, it's us. Your cousins. We were looking for you."

"Paul, Andy and Lorand! I cannot believe it! We didn't see each other in a long time. I believe it was my last birthday the last time we've met. How are you? Oh, I missed you all so much, I am so happy to see you all! You grew so much in one year" said Victor with admiration in his voice.

"Hey everybody, here are my cousins! This is Paul, the big brother, this is Andy, the middle one, and Lorand, the youngest. Paul is 11, Andy is 10, like me, and Lorand will be 9 tomorrow" Victor continued. "We grew up together and they used to come to our home on weekends to play together. We had so many toys, they were everywhere! My mom let us play with all of them!"

Khalifa landed gently on the ground. The Roc bird landed closely to Khalifa. The boys slid down on her left wing, laughing hard. Everybody could hear their jubilant "Wahoo" and laughter.

Victor hugged and kissed them. They held each other for a few seconds, but for Sanda it seemed to be hours of joy. She was waiting for a long time to see them together again.

Sanda knew that her sister is somewhere around. She loves her so much and she wanted to tell her that. Sanda has been trying to find her sister for a year. One day, Gabriela and her family just went away. She was nowhere to be found.

The past came back to Sanda. It was like everything happened just yesterday. She remembered everything.

It was Victor's and Lorand's birthday. Victor was 9 years old and Lorand was 8. One year and one day difference between their birthdays. Sanda and Gabriela wanted to celebrate their children's birthdays together. Sanda was happy to prepare a surprise party for her baby and her youngest nephew. They had a great time. The boys were playing with Ioana and Mihai, the children of their cousin Dana and her husband Vali. There was lot of food on the table, and of course two big cakes with 9 and 8 candles on them. Victor and Lorand were so happy to make their wishes and to blow their candles. Other kids from the neighborhood came over for the party too. There were Radu and Rada, the children of Sanda's best friend Mary and her husband Big Radu. There were also Anca and Alex, the children of her other best friend Mona and her husband Nichola.

The children were laughing and playing. That's all there was, laughter and happiness. Mickey, Victor's cousins' father, asked the kids to say a poem that they learned in school. Paul started to say a poem about a little pussy cat. Then Andy, Lorand and Victor said a poem. Victor said a very short poem:

"Pardon me,
I thought you have a coat.
And I wanted, dear kitty,
To hang your fur on the door"

They all laughed when they heard the cute poem.

The parents clapped their hands. They felt so proud for their children's performances.

When the party was over, before Gabriela and her family left, Sanda was told bad news. Her sister with her family will leave for a year, but they would not tell her where they were going. This broke Sanda's heart.

Here, today, in this magic world, Sanda looked behind her and saw her sister.

With tears in her brown eyes, Sanda ran to her sister and said:

"Oh, my dear. I've missed you much! I am so happy to see you here."

Gabriela gave her a big hug and wiped off Sanda's tears.

"I have missed you too, my dear sister" Gabriela said. "That was the time when my husband wanted to remember how to be a child again, how to be innocent. The best place for him to remember was his childhood hometown. We had a great time. It was one year full of laughter; we played with our kids' every day. Please forgive me because we left without letting you know where we are going. Mickey was in rush to

31

go to that very special place where he grew up, where he was happy. He thought that he forgot how good it is to be a child again, but he realized that he didn't. Look at him now. He is flying a griffin enjoying every moment. His heart is pure, and it will always be."

Gabriela and Sanda looked up and saw Mickey laughing while the griffin was flying in circles. They started to laugh and hold hands. Victor and his cousins looked at them, and they knew that the family is back together. Alex, Victor's father, hugged Gabriela and kissed her rosy cheeks.

"We've missed you" Alex said. "Victor missed his cousins very much."

"We've missed you too…every day" Gabriela said. "We are all happy and nothing can ever change that. I can't wait to tell you everything!"

"Hey, Mickey, you seem like you are enjoying your ride" Sanda called to her brother-in-law.

"Hello, hello. Just give me a second to figure it out how to land this thing. I'll be right there."

"Just think about landing and the griffin will know what to do" Sanda replied.

In the next second the griffin was landing beside them. He bowed gently and helped Mickey slide on his tail. When Mickey touched the ground, the griffin kicked him gently with his tail, and started to laugh.

"Why did you do that?" Mickey asked the griffin.

"Just to remind you that I am not a "thing"" the griffin said. "Ha-ha-ha… oh, it felt good! I told you at the beginning of your ride that this will happen if you forget things…ha-ha-ha."

"Yeah, thanks. Sorry!" said Mickey, also laughing.

"Wow, it's amazing here! I love every moment and I am so happy to be here. We've missed you so much" Mickey said.

Then he looked at Alex and said:

"Hi Alex. Long-time no see. I hope you are well."

"Thank you, Mickey. We are well and were wondering about you. I am happy to hear about the good times you've had with your family" Alex said and then he turned around to the kids.

"Victor, here is your uncle Mickey" Alex said to his son.

Victor and his cousins looked their way. They started to run to the parents. When they got there, big hugs were shared between them.

"What were you flying, uncle?" Victor asked.

"This is a griffin, my dear. Do you know what a griffin is?" Mickey asked.

"No, uncle."

Victor looked at the griffin and saw an animal with the body, tail, and back legs of a lion, the head and wings of an eagle, and eagle's claws as its front feet. *"What bird is that with four legs or what is this animal with wings and beak? Strange thing…"* he was wondering.

GRIFFIN

"Father, please let me tell him everything you told us about a griffin" Paul said.

"Yes, please do" Mickey said. "And don't forget to tell him about the treasures."

"Of course not, this is the best part!" Paul said.

"Victor, a griffin is a lion and an eagle, a legendary composite creature. We know from the legends that during the Persian Empire, the griffin was seen as a protector from evil, witchcraft, and slander. Because the lion is the king of the animals and the eagle is the king of birds, the griffin is thought to be an especially powerful and majestic creature".

"Griffins were known for guarding treasures and priceless possessions. My father chose the griffin today to protect his treasure, which is all of us. Right, dad?"

"Right, my son. My family is my treasure." Mickey said.

"Also, griffins were said to lay eggs in holes on the ground and these nests contained gold nuggets. They are mythical creatures and very devoted to us. We love our griffin! His name is Dusktail."

"Wow…this is amazing! So Dusktail is a griffin in the Magic Wonderland; which animal is he in our world?" Victor asked.

"He is our dog, Tutu. He is a white hunting dog, Lorand said. He likes to sleep beside my bed, and he is always facing the door during the night. It's like he is protecting me…ha- ha-ha…protecting me from what? I have my brothers in my room and they take care of me…ha-ha- ha… My mom said that our great- grandma had a dog with the same name. He was always with my mom, everywhere she went. He wouldn't leave her side. Sorry, aunt, but he didn't love you too much… ha-ha- ha."

"I know that" Sanda said. "Every time we spent our summer holidays to her farm, Tutu was always beside my sister. I knew that he didn't care too much about me, so I always went with my sister around the farm to play with our friends…and I felt safe with my sis and Tutu."

"Across the road of our grandma's house, there was a very old grain mill, and the owner had a little pussy cat. Once I was playing with her, and after a while she bit my hand. Our grandma cleaned the wound and put a bandage on my hand. Tutu has seen everything and from that moment he wouldn't leave my side.

He wanted to protect me from that little pussy cat" Gabriela said.

"Sis, do you remember her farm? "Sanda asked Gabriela.

"Oh, yes, the nostalgia of those days fills up my heart. Do you remember her tiny blue house, made of clay, with a big attic upstairs? I always wondered what secrets she had hidden there. She used to bring old books for us, and she told us to read them. We would hid in the big cherry tree that grew beside her house. We ate the cherries, and most of the time we forgot about reading."

"Then she came asking us very gently to stop eating cherries, because she just baked bread with fried cabbage and butter plum jam inside. Do you remember her stove made of clay and bricks? She used to make huge breads in there and they were so gooood!" Sanda said. "I remember I always wanted slices of bread covered with a thin layer of butter, and fresh tomatoes from her garden...so good..."

"She was so good with us. She always wanted to ensure that we eat what she cooked for us. And we ate everything, didn't we?" Gabriela said. "Beside her little house, she had a huge garden with veggies, corn field and fruit trees: walnuts, plums, pears, cherries, apricots... And there were so many kids coming from all over the country to spend their summer holiday with their grandparents in that village. Every morning, they came to our farm gate and called us to go out to play."

"And our playground was at the old mill, across the road. It was a two-hundred-year-old mill, and the small river that was there made the mill run. The people made white and corn flour! The smell was incredible. Our grandma used to grind her grains there too, and she would came home with sacks of white flour. She made us cookies, cakes, and homemade bread … it was so delicious" Sanda said.

"We used to go in the back of the mill in a flower landfill, play in the little river, and sleep on the grass with wildflowers all around us. Good times!" Gabriela remembered.

They could talk endlessly about their memories, but today was their children's day.

"Go and play now" Gabriela said. "Today is your day. We will go for a walk in the park. You know where you can find us."

A huge park opened right there: green grass, colourful flowers, small trees all around, little benches on the shadowed alleys, water fountains, and many children and parents playing and feeding the animals and the birds.

ROC BIRD

"What kind of bird are you riding today?" Victor asked his cousins. "She is gigantic. Is she for real?"

"Oh, this is Rona, our chicken" Paul said. "We got her when she was only a baby chicken. She goes with us everywhere. When we arrived here this morning, we asked her to be the biggest bird, so we all can ride her together. "*I will be the Roc bird*", Rona told us. She spoked to us for the first time, and mom said that in this world all animals can talk and read our minds. It's amazing, isn't it?"

"We don't know what a Roc bird is, but for sure we all can ride her at the same time" Lorand said. "She is so gentle and kind to us."

"Khalifa, what is a Roc bird?" Victor asked

"My friend, the Roc bird is a bird born from myth and legends. She is very strong and can lift in her nest a full-grown elephant or an adult to feed her babies, legends say" Khalifa said.

"There was a legend of a 10-foot-tall bird that went extinct somewhere in the ancient times. People believed that this bird was ferocious and carnivore, but the Roc Bird was completely earthbound and survived on fruits rather than people and elephants. I have once met a Roc bird, and we laughed so hard about the mythology created around its existence. People created scary stories about everything they were afraid of, and in her case, they were afraid of her size. Ha, ha, ha... It was the most gentle and lovable bird ever. And she is not extinct. She is very alive and will always be."

"Where is she now?" the kids asked

"She is wherever you want her to be. She is immortal like all of us. You just think about her, and she appears" Khalifa said. "And if you look closely, she is right here, right now with you."

"But she is a chicken" Andy said. The expression on his face showed confusion in his mind.

"Yes, she is a chicken in your real world, but here is the Roc bird, the way I know her. I hope this make you understand how the laws of universe work in this imaginary world.

Now, please let me explain to you what this world really is" Khalifa continued. "You see, this world is all around the world. Wherever there is a Wonderland place, there is a portal like this one, which brings the children and their parents to the same place, inside this Magic Wonderland. That is why you've already met children from all over the world. Here, there are no frontiers, and the same language is spoken by everyone, the language of the heart. You can speak in your language, and everybody understands what you are saying."

Khalifa turned around and greeted the Roc bird.

"I am honoured to see you again, my old friend. I can see that you serve these children."

"The honour is mine. I have the time of my old life. These children are all that I needed" Rona said in a sweet soft lady voice. "When I went to them last year, I knew that a new great adventure started."

"Are there many birds like you?" Lorand asked Rona.

"Of course, they are everywhere, but the people must believe to see us. We are the fruit of a legend, and legends never die, and neither do we."

"Wow, it's incredible!" said Lorand in disbelief.

FIREBIRD

"Nice bird you have there" a girl said to Victor's cousins. "Do you like mine? It's a Firebird."

The boys looked in her direction and saw a big bird with feathers and wings made of fire. The girl was riding behind the bird's neck holding on to the flames.

"My name is Daniella" the girl said. She has long, curly blond hair and blue eyes.

Her dress was bright red with orange and yellow lines in it, and it looked like it blended into the bird's flames.

"I am Paul, and these are my brothers, Andy and Lorand. The boy in short blue pants is my cousin Victor. Today is his birthday. Tomorrow is my youngest brother Lorand's birthday."

"Happy birthday!!" Daniella said. "Where are you from?"

"We are from Transylvania" Paul replied. "And you?"

"I was born and raised in Ireland. My parents have a little castle on top of the hill. The view is amazing. I spend my days playing with my goats, Sirin and Lila."

"And how did you get the firebird?" Lorand asked. "What's her name?"

"Her name is Sirin, and she is one of my goats. Lila is that cute blue dragon over there. My cousin Andrew rides it."

"What do you know about your firebird? Was she born in a legend too?" Andy asked.

"My mom told me what she knew from her father. She described the bird as a large one with majestic feathers that glows brightly emitting red, orange, and yellow flames. That's why I chose this dress today, Daniella said proudly. My mom said that the feathers do not cease glowing if removed, and one feather can light a large room if not covered. She also said that there are more stories around my magic firebird, but I do not know them."

"Khalifa, do you know more stories? Can you tell us, please?" Victor asked.

"Of course. Come here all of you and hold my wings. I will take you on a journey where you will see these stories."

"Hey everybody, come over here!" Paul yelled. "Touch these wings and we will go on a special journey!"

"Wait, wait!!" Some children said. "Just wait, we are coming. Victor, Paul, Lorand, Andy!!!!" said the children in unison.

Victor and his cousins looked in that direction. There was a dragon, a Unicorn with wings and a fire-breathing dragon coming towards them. They could see two children riding each creature. *Who are they?* The boys wondered. They looked at each other, but they didn't know the answer. They were too far, and they didn't recognize their voices.

When they got closer, they saw Ioana and Mihai riding the fire-breathing dragon, Anca with Alex were riding the Unicorn, and Rada with her brother Radu were riding the second dragon.

"Hi!! So good to see you all. We've missed you guys" Andy said. "How did you find us here? There are so many children and animals around. It is a crowded day."

"No worries" Rada said. "We just told our riding friends to find you and here we are!"

They landed close to them and wished Victor and Lorand happy birthday.

"I believe we arrived right on time" Mihai said. "We will hear stories about the Firebird. Did I hear that right? After that, we will tell you everything we know about our friends: the dragon, Unicorn, and the fire-breathing dragon. Lastly, we will eat something. I am starving!"

"I am starving too" Andy said." Can we eat first and then play and listen to the stories? I could eat all the cakes from here and I would still be hungry!" said Andy, touching his tummy looking at all the goodies around.

"You all can eat when we arrive in a different world. You will be able to take anything you want from the tables, and we will start to discover the ancient worlds of legends and mystic, my darlings, and now, do not forget to touch my wings" Khalifa said.

"Which tables? Where is the food? I am hungry!" Andy said.

"Just wait a little. The food is there, where we are going" Khalifa said.

Many children came to touch Khalifa's wings, and, in a flash, everybody was in a different beautiful place.

"Hold on now" Khalifa said. "There are different stories about the Firebird. When I tell you the stories, you will see them on a big screen. Make yourself comfortable and just watch."

In an instant, a huge screen appeared before their eyes. The children looked amazed at it and started to clap their hands. Their parents were close by, enjoying the view.

Long tables with luminous raylike vegetables, nectar flowing from glorious fountains of light, and lots of different foods appeared in front of their eyes. Plates were nicely arranged on the tables, along with cups, and chairs. All children and parents took a sit, filled their plates with what they wanted, and started to eat while watching the screen.

Khalifa started to talk softly:

> "Once upon a time there was a modest and gentle orphan girl named Mariuca who lived in a small village somewhere in Transylvania."

Children looked at her sitting on a tree root in the shade.

> "She loved to spend her time there singing. And she loved her village more than anything."

Her voice was the most wonderful in the whole world. The birds stopped singing when she sang, like they've lost their voice. They just sat beside her quietly and listened.

People from around the world heard about her voice and they came from far away to hear it.

Many merchants asked her to go with them and sing for them. She told them she will sing only for the people in her village, and she would never leave the village of her birth.

In a faraway land, there was a sorcerer named Dracol. His younger brother lived in Mariuca's village, but nobody knew he was a sorcerer. His names were Remus. He also loved everybody in the village and helped them when they were in need. He spent days just listening to Mariuca sing and started to fall for her. Mariuca saw Remus helping people, always being kind to everyone, and secretly, she fell for him too.

Remus heard from Dracol that he planned to take Mariuca in his kingdom, to sing only for him. Dracol was clever, and he started to make a vicious plan. He transformed himself into a beautiful young man and visited her. Dracol tried many times to tempt Mariuca by offering to make her Queen if she would sing for him alone, but she refused saying she never wanted to leave her village.

Remus knew that his brother will not stop until he will get what he came for. One sunny day, Remus went to Mariuca and said: "Come with me, the queen of my heart. I will not give you riches, and I will not lock you in a tower to sing only for me. I will give you freedom so you can sing. I love the villagers so much, and I will give them pearls from my tears, so they can buy food or whatever else they need. We will be two free birds, and our feathers will light the villagers' roads or houses. I will be beside you, and I will always protect you."

Mariuca was so happy to hear that the man she secretly loves will let her sing in the village she loves so much. She came up close to him, and they kissed. When their lips touched, they transformed into two beautiful Firebirds. They are still in that village, flying free, one of them singing, and the other one providing pearls and light."

The children were listening to the story, and on many faces a few tears were rolling down. They were happy for the orphan girl having such a happy ending.

Sirin has seen the tears on the children faces and said:

"The honorable King of the Small Animals Realm, please let me tell them the story that I like the most.

47

This has a happy ending too, and I am sure they will love it."

"Do you want to tell the story of the Firebird and Princess Esmeralda?"

"Yes, my dear friend" Sirin said.

Khalifa moved away a few steps making room for Sirin to tell the story.

"In this legend, an archer is on a hunt for a firebird's feather. He wants to give it to the princess that he loves" Sirin started.

"The archer had a very wise and old, devoted dog, who could talk his master language. They spent most of the nights just talking by a campfire. They talked about everything, but mostly about Princess Esmeralda. When the archer saw her the first time, he was in love.

He wanted her heart to be his, but he was too shy to even look at her when she was walking by her castle, so he just loved her from distance.

One day, walking in the woods, he found the most wanted Firebird feather. He wanted to give it to the princess, hoping that she will fall for him, but the soldiers of Vlad, the cruel king of their realm, took it from him and brought it to Vlad. The King ordered the archer to be brought to his castle to reward him. When the archer arrived at the castle, he saw that Princess Esmeralda was sitting beside the King. He didn't understand why, but he didn't ask. His wise dog advised him not to say a word until he is asked.

The King wanted Princess Esmeralda to be his Queen, but she was very smart and had a plan. She knew about the archer's dog being wise, and she heard him giving advice to the archer. She knew that the wise dog would do anything to protect his master. She refused to marry the king until the archer jumps from the highest tower of the castle.

Princess Esmeralda was confident that the archer will ask his dog for his advice. She pretended that she wants to be the only on in the realm to possess a Firebird feather, and to light her chambers. She didn't want the archer to go into the woods and bring more.

The archer begged to see his dog before he would jump, and the dog put a spell on the archer to protect him from falling, but instead to land safely and become very handsome. The dog knew that the King will be jealous, and he will want to be young and handsome too.

The archer jumped and came out more handsome than anyone had ever seen. When the King saw this, he jumped from the tower as well, expecting the same. Instead of coming out young and handsome, there was nobody to save him.

The archer was chosen to be King, married the princess and they lived happily ever after. They still live happily ever after, and they always will."

"Nice story, isn't it?" Sirin asked

"What is the name of the archer, please?" Andy asked.

"Robin"

"And his dog's name?" children asked.

"Azarak. This is the name that the archer chose, and the dog loved it."

"Is there a meaning of the name Esmeralda?" Paul wanted to know.

"Yes, my dear. Esmeralda means *"Emerald"*, which is a precious gemstone" Sirin said.

"Just imagine a dark room filled with bright light only from one feather. Can you believe it?" Sirin asked the children.

"Yes, we do. Can we try with one of yours?" a naughty boy asked.

"My dear, my feathers are not to be shared or hunted. What you heard is the history of our Firebirds family, as it was seen by people during the thousands of years."

"Thank you, Sirin. Thank you, Khalifa" children said in unison.

"There are many more stories and legends. But it's enough for now. Go and play" Khalifa said. "We will talk about more stories later. There are more mythic creatures that you must know about, and next time you will be here, you will learn much more."

FLYING HIGH

"Let's find out which one of our animals flies the highest and fastest" Rada said. "I can bet my dragon is faster and can fly higher."

"Yeah, sure, my Firebird does that" said Daniella with pride in her voice.

"My Roc bird is the best" Lorand said.

"I have never heard about a flying lion, but I trust Khalifa, and I am sure he knows what he is doing, because I don't. Let's have a race and may the best one win" Victor replayed.

All children climbed on their animals, aligned at the starting point, and waited for the sign to fly.

"Listen to me, children" Gabriela said. "I will start to count from one to three. At three you will start to race. No cheating! Do not push the children around you. To make it more entertaining, you will have a quest. I will tell you a riddle, you must decipher it and find the object in it. The first one to find it will be in an instantly returned back here and pronounced as the winner. All the other children will have to ride back."

"What is the prize?" Tannis asked.

"The winner will get a gold star for today and can go to all realms in here. And one more thing: your animal friends are not allowed to tell you the answer. You can ask them where to go but this is all. Understood?" Gabriela asked.

"Yes" said the children with disappointment in their voices.

"Ok, the riddle is:

"Runs, but cannot walk,
Sometimes sings but never talks.
Lacks arms, has hands.
Lacks a head but has a face."

"When you get on top of the highest mountain, right there, there is an old rusty cage with something inside. You must know how to open the cage to get the object to get it back. How you open the cage is your choice, but your devoted riders cannot use their force. Here is another trick: if you can't decipher the riddle, you will not see the object inside the cage. Good luck to all. Now: One, Two, Three!!"

All children with flying magical animals started to fly up high. All of them had the same speed.

But who will win? the parents were wondering looking at their children competing for a special prize.

It's a long flight until the children can reach the top of the mountains. They must fly over an enormous lake in the middle of a very thick forest.

Until they reach the lake, a landfill of coloured flowers delights their view.

In the middle of the garden, there is a wide water fountain covered with rubies. In the sunlight, the rubies are extremely bright, and the fountain looks like water on fire. The water has rainbow colours with sparkling red from rubies. There is a snake made of precious stones that surrounds the fountain, and from its mouth rainbow water comes out onto the field.

A tiny rainbow-river found its way all around the garden watering the flowers. Big precious stones are in the river. They make the water splash onto the flowers, trees, and grass. When the water touches the petals, the flowers change their colour. The grass stays green, and the tress dance in delight of the fresh water.

The snake has his body curled around the fountain. It is said that the snake protects the rubies and comes alive when somebody has a naughty thought to take one as a souvenir. The water is enchanted and keeps the flowers always fresh and the grass bright green.

The legend says that the greatest sorcerer's name Merlin created the garden and used magic to keep it beautiful forever. During the night, all the flowers glow, the trees are purple, and are singing heavenly songs, and the grass is deep blue. It's a spectacular view that takes your breath away. Everything in the garden is constantly changing. The splendor is infinite.

The children are amazed by the beauty of the garden. A fresh flowery wind is blowing in their hair.

When they fly above the lake, a "Wow" from children is heard from far away. The water is crystal clear and is changing the colours from blue to green, and then to transparent crystal clear. They can see the bottom of the lake. Beautiful fish of all colours, with irradiant sparkling lights on their little wings and tails, are swimming all around.

Their parents knew that the mermaids with bracelets made of the thousand- petaled lotus of light waved to their children. Sea horses of the size of real horses, with their cute face, were laughing and welcoming the children to play, waving their cute tails.

The children waved back, and they continued to fly to the mountains. They knew that they must finish the quest first, concentrating on the riddle.

From far, the parents have seen that all children arrived on top of the mountain. Their flying mythical creatures stayed aside on a cliff. They were wondering what is happening there.

All children were on top of the mountain. A rusty empty cage was right there, but they knew that they must decipher the riddle in order to see what is inside. By now, none of them could figure it out.

They were all there looking at the empty cage.

"You have to believe in order to see" Radu said.

"Yes, but this is different" Mihai said. "We have to find the answer first and then we will see."

"The riddle is: 'Runs, but cannot walk, sometimes sings but never talks. Lacks arms, has hands; lacks a head but has a face'" Victor said.

"What can run but cannot walk?" Andy was wondering.

"What can sing but never talks?" Rada asked.

"It has hands but no arms, it has a face but lacks a head" Paul said. "It is weird, isn't it? What can it be?"

"I know, I know!" Victor said

"Me too, me too!" said all the children.

"It is a clock!" they all said at the same time.

At that moment, a crystal pyramid appeared inside the cage with a little gold clock in it. The hands of the clock were standing still, showing the time: 10 in the morning. Two gold antennas attached to the clock came out at the back of the pyramid. The clock had a big happy face with big blue eyes. It was alive.

"What's that?" Lorand asked

"We do not know yet. Let's first figure it out how to break the cage and get the clock" Mihai said.

Victor took a stone from aside and hit the cage. The cage broke in pieces.

"How did you know to do that?" Ioana asked.

"I didn't know it will work. I only knew that the cage is old and rusty, and I tried to break it, and it worked. Yay!!!" Victor said looking amazed at the splendor of the clock.

The rainbow colours were reflected by the crystal pyramid on the clock. The clock's face was bright and shiny in the sun light.

"What do we do now?" Paul asked. "My mom said that the finder of the object will be back in an instant and will get the most wanted prize. But we all deciphered the riddle at the same time."

"Yes, you are right, and all of us should be rewarded. I have an idea" Victor said.

"What, what?" children asked.

"Let's touch each other's shoulders and then touch the clock, maybe we will all be deported" Victor said.

The boys and girls touched the shoulders of the other children in front of them. Victor, Rada, Mihai, Paul, Andy and Lorand touched the pyramid. In that moment, the antennas of the clock touched each other sending a loud gong sound. Their friend animals were right behind the children. And in an instant, all of them were back at the starting point.

"Bravo, bravo!" the parents said. "We are so proud of you!"

"Let's go to Mr. Nemo to give you all the golden stars" Gabriela said. "Today, you are all the winners!"

Mr. Nemo heard the gong and came to them with his magic wand.

"Ha-ha-ha! My lovely children. I knew you will all win. You are the bravest. I came in a flash to congratulate you!"

He touched all children's hands and their stars changed to bright gold. A big happy "Wow" was heard from their voices.

Mr. Nemo wears a red tuxedo with white sapphires at the collar. A tall red hat made his long ears look small.

"Mr. Nemo, can we go now to play in the other realms?" Paul asked.

"Of course, my lovely friend. Whenever you want. But there is so much more to see and learn here."

"I believe we will play longer here" Lorand said. "I would like to know more about the legends."

"All sounds good, but first we have to celebrate" Mr. Nemo said and clapped his paws, and, in a flash, glittering confetti was falling from the sky. The children heard the music of a parade coming towards them. They looked in that direction and an orchestra, conducted by a Phoenix Bird, was singing a beautiful song.

Little rabbits performed the instruments with so much dexterity. The choir formed by little red Cardinal birds started to sing:

"You are the winners
The winners you are all
Looking up the mountains
We knew that you won't fall.

Instead of falling, you rise high
On top you found the clock alive
And when you wondered how and why
The clock just sings, and claps arrive.
A golden star appeared just from hollow
On your hands, with pride to follow.

You are the winners
The winners you are all
Looking up the mountains
We knew that you won't fall.
Ha, ha, ha
Ha, ha, ha
We knew that you won't fall."

Many gifts wrapped in shiny coloured papers were held each by a balloon. All balloons have cute faces, little noses, large eyes, a smiley open mouth and two little hands with white gloves.

Each balloon was responsible to ensure that celebrated child get its gift.

One by one, each balloon started to call the name of the child to give his or her gift.

"Victor… said a gold balloon. "Where are you, cutie?

Here is your gift. You can take it home."

"I am right here! Thank you!"

The balloon eliminated the big noisy raspberry and dissolved in thin air.

All children were called one by one and got their gifts, and after that all the balloons burped a big raspberry and returned to the etheric invisibility.

"I have a question, Mr. Nemo" Anca said.

"Yes, dear. Ask."

"What about our parents? Can they get a gold star for today so they can be with us everywhere?"

"You are very bright, my dear. Ha, ha, ha, and you have read my mind. Of course, ha, ha, ha. This was the last surprise. They all have the gold star for today. Yay!!!"

"Yay!!!!" said the children.

PHOENIX BIRD

"Wow, Mom, dad, the choir's song was so beautiful! What kind of bird was the conductor? It had a wonderful melodious voice" Victor said.

The children from all around looked at Victor's parents. They wanted to know as well.

"It is a Phoenix bird" my son. "It is a magical bird" Victor's mom said.

"Can you tell us more about it?"

"Sure, I can. The Phoenix bird is one of my childhood best friends. But I believe she will love to tell you her story. We just must ask nicely, my dears" Sanda said looking at the bird.

"My dear old friend, would you please tell the children the story you told to me and Gabriela? We never forgot it, but I am sure we cannot say it the same way you do" Sanda continued.

"My pleasure, dears. I've missed you both. Good to see you back" the bird said to the sisters in a soft angelic voice.

"So good to see you too" Gabriela answered. "We've missed you more, but we knew that today we will meet again."

Sanda was thinking the same and she was just nodding her head.

The Phoenix bird looked at the children and bowed. He greeted them all with much elegance.

A Phoenix is a magical bird, radiant and shimmering, and she has red and gold feathers, the colours of the rising sun.

"It is my great pleasure, my friends, to tell you everything about me. I said about me, because only one Phoenix bird can live at a time."

There are many things in a lifetime to see and to learn. There are so many children in every generation to teach and show them things that are not available in their everyday world. Every child is so wonderful that we learn from too.

"As you can see, I am a grand bird, with brilliant ruby and gold feathers and I have a melodious and unique voice. Sometimes a halo surrounds me, illuminating in the sky. It can be seen from far, far away. My eyes are blue and shine like sapphires. Yes, I am a beautiful bird, envied by many birds, said the Phoenix with so much pride in her lovely, sweet voice.

I was born when the universe was created. I am God's pet, and I was released to give the people a glimpse of a Gods' powers, to bring peace to the righteous. I know all secrets of life and I have more knowledge than any other creature in this realm or yours.

In my world, every morning at dawn, I like to sing a beautiful song while I bathe in the magical well found at the very edge of reality, as a bridge connects this world to one beyond it. The song is so enchanting that even the gods stop to listen. Everybody can hear me here, like you did when I conducted the choir, as I sang with the red Cardinal birds. In your world, it is not possible. I am a magical bird and I live only in a magical world.

Every thousand of years, measured in accordance with earthly standards of time, I must die. I gather the finest aromatic woods and spices and build a nest. Then I sit on the nest and ignite it with a single clap of my flaming wings. I am consumed by the flames with so much grace. Then, miraculously, I am reborn from my ashes. Some say that I am immortal, and I must say that they are right.

Sometimes, when a good person or a good animal, is very hurt and almost dies, I shed one tear on the wound, and they come back to life. I am everywhere all the time, all around, watching and protecting the good."

"Your song was amazing" Victor said. "I will remember it all my life."

"Me too, me too," said the children.

"What's your name?" Anca wanted to know.

"I am Phoenix, as simple as that. I am unique and I love my name. It was given to me by God."

"Wow" children said in unison.

"You are so beautiful. I love the fire in your feathers" Anca continued with a shy look in her blue eyes.

"Thank you, my lovely friend."

"Now thank the bird and then go to play" Gabriela said. "Meanwhile, we will enjoy our walk in the garden."

"Thank you, thank you" said all children and then they gathered in a large group with their riders beside them.

They started to talk loudly, and Gabriela heard their laughter while she was walking to the gardens of fragrant flowers and indescribable beauty, where Sanda was waiting for her.

HAPPY MOMENTS

When Gabriela looked towards Sanda, she saw her sister surrounded by many people. She saw them hugging and laughing. And then, a soft guitar song was heard in the realm. Gabriela stopped walking, listened and she recognized the song. She knew Nichola is there.

Wherever Nichola went, he never left behind his guitar. The way he plays, is magical. His voice is soft and touched the souls of his friends and of many strangers also. It happened many times when Nichola was with some friends on the shore of the blue ocean, and he started to sing. People around came closer to listen to him. And Mona, his wife, always sang with him. They complemented each other like the sun with its rays.

Gabriela saw Nichola approaching the group of parents from an alley behind them. His wife Mona, and his father Tic were with him.

Dana and Vali, Mary and Big Radu were laughing and hugging with Sanda, Mickey, and Alex. They are so happy to see each other again. Gabriela and Nichola with his wife arrived at the same time. The hugs and kisses continued. They are so happy. Nothing could cloud this moment. The best memories engulfed their hearts.

"I knew you are here" Gabriela said to Nichola. "I heard your guitar and your voice. I am so happy to see you again!"

"We are happy to see you all!" Nichola said. "We couldn't miss today. It is especially important for all of us and for our children. Look at them. They are having the time of their life!"

"I am so thirsty" he continued. "Is there anything to drink?"

"There are many fruit nectars freshly squeezed" Sanda replied. "Also, the water from the water fountains is cold and refreshing. Just think of what you would like to have, and you will have it in your hand."

Instantly, a gold cup with fresh water appeared in Nichola's hand. He drank it at once. The satisfaction on his face made everybody around to laugh.

"I told you it's good" Sanda said.

"I never had such delightful liquid" Nichola said. "Is this ambrosia? I heard about it. It is sweet and it has a unique perfume. I want one more cup, please."

The golden cup was filled with water, and he drank it without breathing.

"Dad, would you like some?" Nichola asked his father Tic.

"Of course, I wouldn't miss it. Thank you" Tic said, and he drank a big golden cup of delicious water. "Wow, it is really gooood!"

"I can sing again. My throat is not dry now. Mona, darling, today we will have a concert in this gorgeous park. Let's go in the shade and sit on the grass. Today we will sing for our friends."

"Wait for us!"

A voice was heard from the distance. From behind a water fountain, a couple was rushing towards them. They were holding hands.

Sanda and Gabriela had tears of joy in their eyes. They saw their parents coming to celebrate this wonderful day with family. Ionica, Dana's father, was right there beside them.

"Mom, dad, Ionica. Take it easy, do not run. We are waiting for you" Gabriela said.

Nastasia and Grigore, Victor's grandparents, came to them with open arms and big smiles on their faces. Big hugs and kind words of appreciations were shared.

"We need to drink some water, please. The same that Nichola had. We heard him enjoying it" Nastasia said. "Today is a hot day and we are so thirsty."

"No problem. Just think of it and you will have it" Sanda replied.

Grigore, Nastasia and Ionica had their gold cups in their hand, and they started to drink.

"Oh, yeah! This is the best water I ever had" Nastasia said. "I do not remember it being so good when I had it before. Girls, do you remember when we used to bring you here? Magical moments…"

"Magical moments indeed" Grigore said with a shaky voice and tears in his eyes.

"Of course, we remember. We remember everything. Now it's our children's turn to fill their hearts with wonder. They started to feel the magic already and they love it!" Sanda said.

"Let me offer you something comfortable to sit on" Gabriela said to their parents. Four thrones made of bright colourful flowers appeared in front of their eyes.

"These thrones are for my parents, my uncle Ionica and Tic. You are the ones who brought us here from the time we were little children. You are the ones that had trust in us; you kept ours and your hearts kind and open. You all deserve to sit on thrones" Gabriela said. "We cannot thank you enough for everything you have done for us and for our children. You are the Queen and the Kings of our hearts, and we love you very much."

"Yes, yes" they all agreed.

"We will all sit right here in front of you" Mona said. "Let's have some food and drinks."

A long wood table, splendidly carved, with food and cakes, was in an instant in front of their parents. Long benches were on the other side of the table. Everybody took a seat and looked at Nichola. He knew that they want him to play his guitar. While gently his fingers touched the cords, a soft song came alive. It was heard everywhere. Many people from around came closer to listen.

"This song is dedicated to our parents and to all parents in the world" Nichola said.

Nichola started to sing a song about parents. This song was a prayer to God to keep all parents young and beautiful and wishing them to live forever. It was very touchy, and many people had tears in their eyes.

FIRE-BREATHING DRAGON

When children heard Nichola singing, they came running to their parents.

"I knew we'd all be together today" Victor said. "This was one of my birthdays wishes! Thank you, Khalifa."

"Mine too" said Lorand.

"Anytime, my little friend. Your wish is my command" Khalifa said with a humble voice.

All children came to their parents and listened quietly to the music of the strings. When Nichola ended the song, the children ran to their grandparents. Big hugs and kisses just melted their hearts.

"Hi grandma, grandpa" Victor said. "I am happy you could come today. Oh, I love your thrones. Are they comfy?"

"Very comfortable and they smell so good" Grigore said.

"Who could imagine that a chair can smell heavenly?" Ionica said. "Mine at home don't smell so good."

"Mine neither" Tic replied.

"Neither ours, but hey, here everything is possible" Grigore said.

"Kids, what do you want to do now?" Mona asked.

"Ioana and Mihai want to tell us the story of their pet, the fire-breathing dragon" Alex said. "And then, I want to tell them about our Unicorn!"

"I want to tell the story of our dragon!" Rada continued. "They are fascinating creatures."

"OK, do you want to do it here?" Mona asked them.

"Yes, of course, if you all are alright with that?" Alex answered.

"Of course, come over here."

The grandparents had their grandchildren on their knees. All the other children came closer to hear the stories.

"Mihai, would you please start to tell the story of our dragon? You are the storyteller in the family" Ioana continued.

"My dear friend, please introduce yourself" Mihai addressed to his fire-breathing dragon.

The fire-breathing dragon is a gorgeous creature. Everybody could see that she is a lady, with bronze body and giant teeth and claws, huge purple wings, long eye lashes and bright purple lipstick on her lips. She has a smile on her face that touched the hearts of her audience.

"My name is Nyre" she said with a soft and sweet voice "and I am so pleased to give a ride today to these two wonderful children."

"Nyre, now please sit beside me and help me to tell the truth about your kind" Mihai said.

Nyre sat beside him with her tail around her body.

"Legends of fire-breathing dragons have fascinated people for centuries and appeared in cultures all over the world throughout history. Like all mythical creatures in this realm, Nyre was born in myths and legends. It seems possible that all these legends might have been based on a real creature. Nyre is proof that the fire-breathing dragons are real.

Unfortunately, in all stories, these dragons were hunted and killed by people. In legends, the fire-breathing dragons were described as ferocious. It is not true though." Mihai said.

"How do you know it's not true?" Victor asked.

"Because I asked Nyre and she told me that. I believe her with all my heart. The animals do not lie."

"In our legends from Transylvania, the fire dragons were the dragons that were each responsible for a different element of the earth. The fire-breathing dragons are responsible for fire, they symbolize energy and teach people to overcome obstacles with courage."

"It takes courage to ride her, right? Nyre is 50 meters long, she is impressive" Mihai said.

"When you look at her, for sure you don't want to make a move to make her angry, but she is so gentle, kind, and so funny too. Just looking into her eyes, we have courage for everything and know without a doubt that she is here for us. Kiss, kiss, Nyre. We love you" said Mihai blowing kisses to Nyre with his tiny hand.

Nyre started to smile shyly; everybody could swear that she was blushing.

"Let me tell the last story, please, and then we go to play" Ioana asked her brother.

Mihai stepped back and made room for Ioana to come in front of everybody.

With a confidence in her voice, Ioana said:

"Once upon a time, there was a great dragon - very fierce and strong. It was this dragon that burnt all the deep dark woods in Transylvania. Magnificent forests they must have been, but the dragon set them on fire with his burning breath. Men were so scared of her, and women ran away when her shadow crossed the skyline.

The fire-breathing dragon made the whole land a desert. The people called her "Bruta" which is "The Beast".

One day, the dragon came close to a town. Bogdan, one of the famous warriors at that time, took with him long and sharp arrows, and then went out to meet the beast.

When he was close to the dragon, he drew his bow. The first arrow shot the beast through the heart.

The dragon was buried on the Feleac Hill, close to the town. There still is the "stone of the beast". Everybody can go and see it even today. It's still there."

"As my brother said, they are sad stories" Ioana continued.

"Were the dragons so frightening in the past?" Anca asked. "She doesn't look at all to be like that. I want to kiss her cheeks right now. She is so lovely" and she waved gently to the dragon.

"No, they were not, my dear. People feared dragons and didn't understand that the dragons respect and protect the four elements of the nature: water, earth, air, and fire. Each of the four elements contains its own unique powers, which work together to create one universe. They are all sacred elements that we must always protect" Nyre said. "Too bad that all of this happened, but we are here in this realm to dedicate our life to the children and to teach them the importance of the four elements."

"Wow, and you protect fire?" Victor asked curiously.

"Yes, I do, with all my heart. There are more dragons that protect the other elements. When something bad happens to these elements outside of this realm, we all go and restore the balance of the nature" Nyre answered.

"Is it easy to do it?" Rada asked.

"Not always, but we always succeed. This is our role in this world and nothing and nobody can stop us. Who would dare, right? Look at my size…ha, ha, ha!" said Nyre as she laughed hard.

"Are there more stories related to your kind?" Lorand asked.

"There are many more from all over the world, but this is enough for today" Nyre answered. "There's Anca and Rada to tell you their stories about their animal friends."

"Thank you, Nyre" said Anca. "I believe is my turn now."

UNICORNS

"Hello everybody, my name is Anca, and this is my little brother Alex, for the ones who don't know us. It is my great pleasure to introduce Pearl, our lovely unicorn with wings.

We have tried to search for myths and legends regarding the unicorns but searching for unicorn myths is like searching for unicorns themselves. What we know is that the unicorn is a pure white horse with a majestic horn upon its forehead, she can fly, and it has massive wings, and for sure is a symbol of wisdom, purity, and chastity. Their horns have magical healing qualities. Unicorns symbolize prosperity and peace.

The unicorns' true origins lie in the depths of time. They descended from the heavens. They are amazing creatures with power beyond imagination. They have the beauty of a stallion, the powers of a god, and the ability to fly like an arrow."

"I wish I could take her home with us" Anca continued. "I know I can't, but we will come often to visit her. Will we, dad?"

"Of course, my dear. Anytime you want" Nichola said. He knew in his heart that the bond was created in between Pearl and his children.

With a smile on her face, Anca continued:

"She is fierce yet good, selfless yet solitary, but always mysteriously beautiful. Unicorns can be captured only by a girl. The unicorns have the fluidity in their movement, they are gracious. They are soft, kind, and emotional creatures. They are the only mythical creature whose origin is not based on human fears. The unicorns are honoured and respected by everyone. They are strong, solitary animals who seek to do good for all around them. Never does a unicorn pose a threat to humans, or any other creature that does not seek first to harm them. It is believed that the unicorn's horn neutralize poison."

"How do you know her name?" Radu asked

"We asked her, and she was kind to let us know" Alex answered. "Anca called for her and she gently came towards us. Pearl, her name fits like a glove to her. Don't you think? She is ivory white like a pearl. Sea pearls and our Pearl are considered to offer the power of love and protection. Sea pearls are thought to give wisdom through experience, while our Pearl is the wisdom itself."

"Anca, you said that you tried to look for myths and legends regarding the unicorns. Did you find any?" Radu asked curiously.

"Yes, we found a few, but I do not want to keep you here. Let's play!"

"There are many legends in Transylvania" Victor said.

"Yes, dear, that land is full of myths and legends, stories of good and evil. It is a magical land" Sanda answered to her son.

"It is a nice story" Lorand said.

"And a long one" Andy continued.

"Long one? It was the shortest story we heard today. Did you get bored, my brother?" Paul asked Andy.

"No, of course not, the story is very interesting, but I am hungry again. Can I eat something now?"

"Sure" Gabriela answered. "Take anything you want from the table. Everything is delicious."

"Can I touch Pearl?" Victor asked.

"Of course. He loves kids" Alex said. "We played all morning."

Victor gently touched Pearl's hair; he brushed it with his fingers.

"Wow, it feels like… happiness. It feels like touching love with fingers" Victor said in awe. "How is this possible? I felt it very strong."

"Yes, my friend" Khalifa said. "This is how it feels when you touch a unicorn. It is magical. Love and happiness run through your veins, and they are eager to give it to everybody."

DRAGONS

"I have the same feeling when I touch my sweet dragon" Rada said.

"I started to wonder if these fantastic stories about our best friends are more than just myths. What if these legends are true?" Victor said.

"They are true" Khalifa said. "They were always true but is very hard for humans to comprehend the reality and they turned them into legends and fantasies."

"Dragons are fantastic animals with such a delicate touch in this world and yet so fearsome in the legends" Victor continued.

"You are so right" Rada said. "They have been hunted and killed by scared people, or just for showing the power over them. It was so wrong."

"The dragons of legend are actual creatures that have lived in the past. They inhabited the earth long before men appeared on earth. At the time, it was said that the dragons were evil and destructive" Rada continued. "Stories of dragons have been handed down for generations in many civilizations. No doubt many of these stories have been exaggerated through the centuries. But that does not mean they had no original basis in fact. During the history, dragons were thought as being like any other mythical animal: sometimes useful and protective, other times harmful and dangerous.

The word "dragon" comes from the ancient Greek word 'draconta', meaning 'to watch', suggesting that the beasts guarded treasure, such as mountains of gold coins or gems."

"My sweet dragon, Goldbert, right here beside me, is not ferocious at all. He has never been. He told me his story" Rada continued.

"He was born in a cave. His mother, the Gold Queen Dragon, died giving birth. His childhood was very hard and sad. He had nobody to play with, nobody to feed him, nobody to keep him warm at night.

In that cave, there were mountains of gold, and somehow, he knew that he had to protect them, because his mom gave birth right there, in that cold cave.

He grew up by himself, eating fruits and leaves from around the cave. There were plenty all year round.

Goldbert felt so lonely, until one day when he saw a little girl, eating wild fruits from the bushes, in front of his cave. He was so happy, and he went to her. When she saw him, she started to run screaming and crying. She was so scared, and she ran inside the cave, thinking that there she will be safe.

And indeed, she was.

Goldbert has seen people coming towards the cave with bats and swords. He knew in an instant that they are after her. He went in the front of his cave roaring hard, and the people started to run away in all directions.

He went inside laughing. The girl stopped crying and she looked at him with her innocent dark brown eyes. She couldn't believe that a dragon could laugh."

"*I am Goldbert*" the dragon told to the little girl. "*What's your name?*"

"*I am Princess Arabella*" she said. Arabella couldn't believe that the dragon is talking to her.

"*Do not fear me*" he said. "*I will protect you. You are safe with me*" the dragon continued. "*Who were those people? They were coming after you, right?*"

"*Yes, they wanted to kill me. They killed my father, the King of this land, and they want to have the power over our people, to take all their money and all their food, and to let them starve.*"

"*So, you are The Princess. I heard about you from people passing by my cave. Your Highness, would you let me help you regain your land, to have peace and to be rich to feed all your people?*"

"*Yes, Goldbert, but I do not know how we will do that. They have a big army surrounding my father's castle.*"

"Are there more bad people somewhere else?"

"I do not know for sure. I heard my father saying that this enemy army is not big but is bigger than ours. Our knights died trying to save me and my father. One of them, the last knight alive but really hurt, he took me out of the castle, and he told me to run as far as I can. I ran all night through the woods and here I am now. I am so happy I've met you. I am not scared anymore."

"We never had a war" the Princess continued. *"There was always peace and happiness in our kingdom."*

"Please eat some fruits from the gold plate over there and try to sleep. Nobody will come to bother you here. I promise" Goldbert said and left.

"Arabella found a bed made from leaves and went to sleep after she ate some delicious fruits. She was very tired. Goldbert went to the castle and waited for the enemy army to fall asleep. The night was dark, and there was no moon light in the sky. The stars were hidden behind the stormy clouds." said Rada.

"I didn't tell you that my Goldbert is the protector of the earth, like Nyre is the protector of fire" said Rada with pride in her voice.

"So, when Goldberg was sure that the enemy of the castle was asleep, he created a tornado with stones and earth that surrounded the castle and killed the army.

A thunderstorm started with heavy rain and their bodies were washed down the mountains.

Next morning was beautiful. The sun was shining and the people from the castle found out that the enemy left, and they were free. The king's treasure was found in chests by the gate.

Goldbert went back to the cave, took Arabella on his wings, and raced to the castle. When the people saw the princess riding a dragon, they were so happy to see her alive and they didn't feel scared by the dragon.

All the treasure from the cave was brought to the castle. The kingdom was very prosperous, all people were happy, and they lived in peace. Goldbert was watching over the castle and helped people in need. And only Arabella knew that her dragon is talking. They spent many nights just talking about everything.

Goldbert was very happy there."

"And now he is happy here too" Radu said.

"Wow, what a nice story... We are so lucky to make friends with such wonderful animals. I would like to come back here someday" Ioana said. "Can I, mom?"

"Of course, dear. This is only the beginning of your journey" Dana said.

"*Blah, blah, blah... everybody did something great... yuck! All animals are great, they have powers, they love children...blah, blah, blah. What about me?* Shadow was thinking. *I am cute, I am smart, but I don't love children, so what? They don't love me either.*"

"*I like to chase them with a wood stick on fire. I want to bite them just a little so they can feel how strong I am. Dragons, unicorns, Khalifa...you are a joke! Do you hear me? I am the most important thing in this realm. My mom told me that I am the best in everything I do. Yes, I am!*"

"*Why are there so many people coming here? It's Victor's birthday... yuck. So what? They didn't come to my birthdays. I do have a gift for you, Victor. Just wait and see. And your precious friend Khalifa will not be able to do anything about this. Hi, hi, hi!!!*"

<hr />

ZAYA AND THE GREAT KRITON

"Mom, I didn't see Zaya yet" Victor said. "She said she will come today!"

"Look right over there, she is talking with a centaur."

"With what?" Victor asked.

"A centaur, darling. He is a mythical creature with the upper body and head of a human and the body of a horse."

Victor and his cousins looked in the direction pointed by Sanda, and they saw their mothers' nanny with a tall half man – half horse.

Zaya was Sanda's and Gabriela's nanny when they were little girls, and she remained their friend since.

"Hello, hello" Zaya said from not too far. "I was here from the beginning, and I heard everything said. But I spent a little time with my new friend here.

Please meet The Great Kriton. He is the greatest centaur that ever existed."

"What is a centaur?" Victor asked with his cute voice.

Zaya smiled and said:

> "It is said that the Centaurs are a creation of a fairy tale in which wild inhabitants of the mountains and cruel spirits of the forests were combined in half-human, half-horse form. Centaurs existed in tribes and made their homes in caves, hunting wild animals, and arming themselves with rocks, tree branches and arrows. Centaurs were creatures that represented chaos and barbarism, and some centaurs only acted in such a way under the effects of wine and alcohol. Centaurs are said to be extremely heavy drinkers and were usually depicted as beasts.

They were thought to carry bows and were very short-tempered creatures. But most Centaurs are good and work against evil.

The most civilised centaur was Kriton, who was incredibly wise, and a tutor and advisor to many heroes. He didn't like to drink; he was very educated in nature."

> "How do you know that much about him, Zaya? Do you know Kriton for a long time?" Victor asked.

> "I've known him for a long time, by the time I used to come here with your mother and your aunt. We spent most of the weekends here and all their vacations" Zaya said. "Kriton told me everything at that time.

He said that he was born in very ancient times, and his father Cronos was the god of the universe. Kriton was and is the wisest centaur on hearth. Also, Kriton is the founder of medical art. Without his hard work, there would be no medicine in the world.

God Apollo adopted Kriton and taught him how to be honorable and enlightened. Apollo trained him in music, poetry, skills in treating wounds, and the mystery of prophecy. He has been injured by one lethal arrow, which was filled with venom. Kriton suffered immense pain. As an immortal, however, he could not die, but he was in great pain. Kriton gave up his own immortality for the good of others. In honor of this noble sacrifice, Kriton's image was placed in the stars. The constellation Centaurus honored his kindness and selflessness. His life ended, but his noble sacrifice is remembered for eternity. And yet, he is here with us. How is this possible, my dear friends?" Zaya continues.

"Do not forget that this is a magical land and magic happens here. Everything is possible here. I am part of this amazing realm and thanks to my friends here, I am immortal again" Kriton said.

Kriton is a very handsome centaur. He has long dark hair with black sparkling eyes. On his shoulder he carries arrows.

"Why do you have the arrows?" Victor asked. "Here is the safest place in the world. Nothing bad can happen here."

"I died with the arrows on my shoulder, and I was reborn with them. Do not worry, my little friend, they are not poisonous, and I removed their heads anyway. I do not want the children to play with them and to get injured themselves. I wear them because they are part of my history" Kriton said.

"Wow…can we see them?" Victor asked.

Kriton gave the arrows to children to look at them.

"They are amazing!" Paul said. "The wood smells so nice and their surface is so smooth and soft. Who made them?"

"I made them" Kriton said. "They were the finest in the world at that time. I thought the Greek Gods to make them too and they were invincible."

"How tall are you?" Lorand asked. "You are taller than my dad."

"I am taller than all humans, but I am not as tall as a dragon…. ha, ha, ha" Kriton said.

"I like you" Lorand continues.

"Do you want to be my friend?" Kriton asked Lorand.

"Mom, dad, is it OK to have Kriton as my friend?"

"Of course, darling. He is our friend too" Gabriela answered.

"OK then, I will be your friend. My mom said it is all right. But you must promise me something" Lorand continued.

"Anything. Just ask and it will be done" Kriton answered with a big smile on his face. He loved to be challenged by the children.

'I need you to teach us how to make the arrows. I want to tell all my friends at school everything about them!"

"It would be my pleasure, my friend, but don't forget that you need magic to make these magical and invincible arrows."

BLUE REALM

Thiassi and Nemo came closer to the group and asked:

"Who wants to go and visit the water realm? You can play with the water; you can swim and make more friends there. There are many water animals that are waiting to play with you."

"Me, me, me!" said the kids in unison.

"Just make sure that your companions come back to their real size and origin. Their majestic sizes might be scary for the animals in the water realm" Nemo continued." Do not worry, their power of protection and communication will be the same."

"Why are they going to the Blue Realm? I can't get there. I am stuck in this Red Realm. It would have been so nice to be able to go there and to pretend that I want to play with Victor and to kidnap him when nobody is looking. Hi-hi-hi... I must wait for them to come in this

*Red Realm, and I will make Khalifa give me his crown.
It will be mine! I will be the King! Hi-hi-hi!!* Shadow
thought from his crystal dome.

In a blink of the eye, the children and their parents were
transported to a wonderful land where the water was bright
and sparkling as diamonds. The gardens around the water have
many gorgeous, coloured flowers and their smell is the most
pleasant like nothing else in the world.

"Khalifa, what flowers are those?" Victor asked.
"They smell so wonderful, even more beautiful than
my mom's roses."

"These are magical flowers" Khalifa said. "Their
fragrance engulfs your body and senses and gives you
the power over the water. You can command the water
and the water will do whatever you ask for."

"That's great!" Victor said.

"Water, please give us a water toboggan" Victor
ordered.

A tall toboggan started to take form, with stairs of water and
the sliding side. The children started to climb the stairs, very
slowly at the beginning, not trusting that the stairs will hold
their weight. When they saw that the stairs were strong enough
for them, they ran up and glide down in the toboggan with
roars of screaming laughter.

"Can I be surrounded by a bubble of water and to fly with it?" Andy asked.

"Just snap your fingers and it will be done" Khalifa said.

Andy snapped his fingers, and a big water balloon surrounded him, and he started to fly around like he was weightless.

"Ha, ha, ha, it's so nice in here. You can see everything around. Come here, guys," said Andy.

The children snapped their fingers, and the balloons lift them up in an instant. They embraced flying with youthful joy and were laughing loudly. Nobody told them that when the bubbles touch one to another, they break, and the children might fall. The parents knew that and silently were waiting to command to the water to support their fall. This happened to them a long time ago and they remembered that it was so much fun.

The breeze of the perfumed air let the children fly slowly around the realm. In a while, a wind started out of nowhere and the water balloons were moving at a faster speed, coming closer and closer together. The children enjoyed it more. When the first two balloons touched, Victor's and Lorand's, a raspberry sound could be heard in the realm when they broke, and the children knew they will fall. Water palms were formed underneath them and landed them slowly.

"I was not afraid" Lorand said. "I knew that the water would protect us."

"How did you know that?" Victor asked him. "Nobody told us."

"Of course, I knew. My mom told me before. She said it's a secret, but she told me everything because I am her youngest son, and she didn't want me to be afraid. So, I was not afraid."

Lots of raspberry sounds could be heard in near distance and the water palms brought the children closer to their parents.

"I would like to have water balls fight. Who is in?" Paul asked.

"Me, me, me" children said.

"Go closer to the water, place your open palms above the water, at your height distance, and the water will come into your palms. You don't have to go to scoop it up. Just think what you want the water to do for you, and the water will grant your wishes" Khalifa said.

The children formed two groups close to the water. They did what they were told and were amazed to see the water coming straight into their palms. With both palms, the children formed the water balls, and they started the fight. Sometimes they hit the target, sometimes they missed, but this didn't matter, they were having so much fun.

Very soon, their clothes were wet, and their faces and hands were shiny from water.

"Let's swim in the water" Mihai said.

"Yes, let's do this" Alex said.

When they wanted to jump in the water, a wonderful surprise made them stop and look speechless to the apparitions at the surface of the crystalline water: mermaids.

Gorgeous and surreal mermaids were sitting on the rocks by the water. They were all looking in their mirror combing their hair in very slow motion. It was unreal. Even after seeing wonders all day, they still couldn't believe their eyes.

MERMAIDS

NERIS

"Hi, dears. We are the nine main mermaids all around the world. Many countries and cultures have their own versions of mermaids, in which we were described as a snake water goddess or a fish with a monkey mouth. I will introduce myself first and then I will let my friends tell you, their stories.

I am Neris, the mermaid continues with the story. As you can see, I am a giant fish with a human face and a monkey's mouth, and I feel pretty, even if the ancient people said that I am not. They didn't see the true me. They tried for so long to catch and eat me because they knew that anyone who eats the Neris will have eternal youth and beauty. But when they came close to me, I had to put my horns and fangs to scare them. They also knew that catching a Neris often brings terrible storms and misfortune to entire villages, so they gave up. Ha- ha- ha, they were fooled by me!

What they never knew is that they could be my friends and I could grant their wishes at any time.

People really believe that we have mystical abilities, and a variety of magical aspects have been attributed to us. For example, we can cry tears of pearls. And yes, we cry pearls, the most expensive ones in the human's world, and they are so rare.

In addition, we can foretell the future. Humans believed throughout the history that we are less compassionate and are capable to trap men into the sea.

We all are magical creatures and we all can do splendid things for our human friends. Unfortunately, this is what the humans in old ages didn't understand. Well, their loss! Luckily, people in this world know the truth and that is all that matters."

"You are as beautiful as my mother, Victor said. I like your blue eyes and blue long hair, and your blue-tinted skin. Is your tail blue as well? How often do you comb your hair? It's so shiny!"

Neris jumped in the water, and she revealed a blue sparkling tail, with blue sapphires on it. There were big red rubies on her belt, along with long earrings made of red rubies. A crown of rubies and sapphires appeared on the mermaid's forehead. Her hair was sparkling in the sunlight. The children, parents and grandparents were amazed by her beauty.

"We all have a magical comb and a magical mirror. And yes, we comb it while we sing our mesmerizing songs" Neris answered kindly.

"Will you sing for us?" Victor insisted. I have read that when the mermaids sang, they were trying to bring sailors into the ocean's depths, or the mermaids just smashed their boats with storms if they didn't feel like putting the effort into being charming" Victor said. "People had to tie themselves or to cover their ears when they were passing by the sirens because their beautiful voices made them jump in the depths of the water and drown."

"There are no threatening sailors or boats here, my friend. The times you speak of are ancient.

It's true, these things sometimes happened, but this was just our way to protect ourselves from being hunted down" Neris answered.

"And to answer you Victor, yes, we will sing for you if you want. You don't have to wax your ears or tie yourselves to the tress around the water. Ha, ha, ha, I can see that this story is still known in these days.

All mermaids are harmless in this realm, and extremely friendly. We are here to serve you and grant your wishes, exactly like your animal friends."

"That's great!" Victor said. "Thank you. I will have my wishes in a bit. Mom, can I ask them to show us Aqualand (Waterland)?"

"You can ask everything, my darling. They can show you the Aqualand, for sure. We visited it too, a long time ago" Sanda answered.

"Can we play with dolphins? I know that they are the most intelligent mammals in the sea" Victor continued.

"They are waiting for you, dear. Just look at them right there" Sanda said.

Many dolphins were jumping happily in the water, speaking in their language, inviting everybody to play with them.

"We will take you there" Neris said. "But first I want you to meet my friends from all around the world."

"This is Terya, the Lady of the Waters. Out of all of us, she is the oldest mermaid. In ancient times, humans knew her as a water snake that attracted sailors to her underwater palace, where they became her husbands.

The mermaids were blamed for many bad things just because the humans didn't know their life in their kingdoms, and it was very hard for them to understand. The same thing happened to your animal friends. Terya is immortal, like all mermaids and all animals in this realm."

"All our kingdoms are prosperous, and we have been living in peace for thousands of years." Neris continued.

"Terya, you have green eyes, green hair, and light brown skin" Ioana said. "Neris is blue. Can you tell me why?"

"My dear, the colour of the skin is just an identification of our kingdoms. We all come from different realms, and yet we are alike. We love people, we like to help those in need, and we save as many sailors as we can, no matter where they are in your world."

"Which colour is your tail?" Ioana asked.

Terya started to swim a little in the water, jumped a few times and her apparition was magical: green hair, green eyes, green tail, and light brown skin. White sapphires enriched her skin, hair, and tail. A small diamond crown on her head made her look like a princess. Collective "Wow" was heard from the crowd. The children, their parents and grandparents were speechless.

"Thank you all for your kindness, Terya said. We are all blessed with beauty in this realm and in our world."

"I wish I will look like you when I grow up" Ioana said. "Or like her, or like her" Ioana said looking at all mermaids around them. "You are all so beautiful."

"Oh dear, of course you will look like us. Beauty comes from inside and I can tell that your heart is bigger than many people have in your world. I know you will be very happy; a son will be given to you and the husband will love and protect you always" Terya said.

"How do you know this?" Ioana asked. "My mom didn't tell me that, and she knows everything."

"We have prophetic powers, my dear. Your mom is the most wonderful mom, but she can't see the future. I can!" Terya said.

"So, you have magic powers?" Ioana asked with her big eyes.

"Yes, I have, like all mermaids in this realm. And I am very pleased to let you know that your beauty will challenge the beauty of a princess in your realm."

"Mom, did you hear? I will be beautiful as a princess!" Ioana said looking at her mom.

"To me and your father, you are the most beautiful princess now and forever" Dana said.

"This is Lira, the "water spirit", and she came from Golf of Guinea. She can sometimes take human form. She likes to heal the wounds of those in need if she is around. It makes her so sad to see anybody hurt." Neris continued.

"How do you heal the wounds?" Victor asked.

"I just touch the wound with my magical tail, and I breathe life in their mouth.

Then, I touch gently their hair and when I see that they are coming back to life, I sing healing songs. A tornado of powerful healing light comes over the wounded body, and in a blink of an eye, they open their eyes, not knowing what happened. They just see me and are happy that they have seen a mermaid. Then I jump back in the water and disappear in the calm waves of the ocean."

"What else do you do?" Paul asked.

"I am known for fertility. I give children to moms and dads."

Lira jumped into the blue ocean, and when she came out, she was sliding slowly on the water with her shiny tail and with hands above her head in a very elegant posture. A low "Wow" sound was heard in the realm. Her beauty was exquisite. Her body and her robe were covered in bright blue gemstones.

"What stones are these, Khalifa?" Victor asked. "They are so beautiful, and I have never seen something like this. They are so bright and shiny."

"These rare gemstones are found in San Benito County, California. This is where they got the name: Benitoite. They emit strong fluorescence and shine in bright blue color" Khalifa said.

"I do not get it. You are from Golf of Guinea and the gemstones are from California. How did you get them?" Mihai asked.

"My dear, I got them from my dolphins' friends here. They collect the precious stones from the seas and bring them to mermaids" Lira said.

"Here is Ecryla, the Guardian of the Seas. Over there is Silky. Beside her is Ella which is the Spirit of the Fresh

Water. Arianna, Star and Ada are the shy mermaids. Ada's family are the "Shapeshifters of the Sea".

"Do not fear me, my darlings. I like to sing and dance with my mermaid friends here. We all can take human forms and enjoy the fields around. We like to hear the birds singing, the trees growing and the animals talking. And most of all, we love to play with water and show the children the amazing life in the depths of the oceans." said Ella.

"We would like to swim in the water, but we cannot stay long underneath the water, we cannot breathe" Victor said.

"We all have the magical power in our hands and if you would like to come and visit our world, we will ensure that you can breathe and swim as fast as all fish in the seas!" Arianna said.

"Mom, dad, can we go, please?" Lorand said.

"Of course. We would like to come too, if this is all right with our friends here" Gabriela said.

"Gabriela, my dear, we had so much fun when you were a child and for sure we will enjoy our time together again. You are all welcome in our world" Arianna said.

"Yay!!" the kids said. "Let's go!"

Khalifa stepped out of the crowd and said:

"Thank you all, dear mermaids. Your stories are as unique as your realms. Children, do you have questions?"

"Yes, yes, yes" said the children in unison.

"OK, let's give the priority to Victor, since today is his birthday" Khalifa said.

"Thank you, my little cat. What do you eat? Do you eat fish?" Victor asked the mermaids.

The mermaids started to laugh with angelic voices.

"Oh no, my darling" Ada said. "The fish are our best friends. We eat algae, leaves of ocean forests, and seaweeds. They are very tasty, give us lots of energy and are very healthy. We never get sick, as humans do. Even if we get wounded by the sea monsters, we recover in an instant."

"Can you talk with fish?" Victor continued.

"Yes, we speak their language, which is the fish language. The smaller the fish, the sweeter the voice."

"Wow, I would like to be able to talk with them too!" Victor said.

"You have this chance every time you are in this realm. You can talk with fish as easily as you can talk with all other magical animals in this land" Ada said. "You see, in this magical land, we all can talk in our tongue, everybody understands and there is no need for translation. The language is unique and very special. The vibrations of anybody voice's sound is understood by all of us no matter where we came from or who we are."

"It is my turn now" Lorand said. "Tomorrow is my birthday. Do you still kidnap humans to be your husbands? Please do not kidnap my dad" Lorand asked Ada with tears in his eyes.

"No sweetie, we have not kidnapped anybody for ages. This happened in ancient times, before the dinosaurs disappeared from earth."

"Ok then" Loran said. His eyes were smiling, and his tears dried in the sun light. "That means that you can sing for us without our dads to be in danger."

"Of course, darling," said Ada.

The mermaids started to swim in a circle that grew smaller and smaller, the water was splashing with bright colours from their tails. Colourful sparkling water fireworks coming out of the ocean's depths, gave a wonderful image to the viewers. Wonderful voices, singing in unison were heard all around. The song was so harmonious, like thousands of angels were singing at the same time. Everybody could feel the smooth vibration of the sounds. It was comforting and tranquil. When they stopped, a soft "Wow" was heard in the realm. Nobody could say a word. They were all speechless.

"Is it true that underneath the water somewhere there is the lost continent of Aqualand? Can we go and visit it?" Paul asked. "I've read about the lost continent. Aqualand means Waterland. My mom said that the word "aqua" means "water". It must be hidden here, right? Does anyone know its location?"

"We know it is still there, and now you know too, my dear. Aqualand always existed in this realm. Nothing is lost. We preserved our culture, knowledge, and treasures. Aqualand was and still is our home" Ada said. "The old teachings and knowledge are stored in Gold City, just for protection."

"Wow, what else is there that we should visit?" Paul asked.

"There are countless civilizations that have not been part of your world for thousands of years, including the underground people who lived in the core of the Earth. Their civilizations are very advanced and only a few ever had a chance to visit them. The few explorers who returned, and published their findings, were ridiculed, and nobody believed them. In fact, they came in our world without knowing what they will find" Ada continued." You may wonder how this could happen, but I will tell you the secret. Can you keep a secret?"

"Yes, yes, yes" the children all eagerly promised at the same time.

"Today is a very special day. The Mighty Council of the Magic Wonderland wants to give this gift to Victor and Lorand for their birthdays, and of course, to all of you here today that also hold the golden star."

"The secret is that there are four portal gates in your world, some say there are more" Ada continued. "Two of them are big openings at the poles that go very deep inside Earth, and they are very dark. Only the brave and pure souls had the courage to explore deeper and deeper beneath the Earth's surface, until they found Pearl City, the land of everlasting mystery. Of course, in their search, they did not see us, the mermaids. They do not know what is in this realm, but some people had a chance to meet the subterranean civilizations.

The third portal is located underneath the pyramids in Egypt, and the fourth one is under Bucegi Mountains in Transylvania."

"Victor, you, and your cousins are originally from Transylvania, right?" Ada asked.

"Yes, we are" said Victor with pride in his voice. "It's very beautiful there. We have majestic Carpathian Mountains, wildlife, and wild berries in the forest. Transylvania is very beautiful. Now we live in Canada, the land of opportunities, as my mom says."

"Today we will visit the underworld civilizations. We do not invite all children to visit them. These realms are only for chosen ones…and you all are the chosen ones today" Ada continued.

NAUTILUS

"Now, come jump in the water and let's start our journey" Khalifa said.

"Can we all come?" Victor's father asked.

"Absolutely. Everybody is welcomed today."

"I can't swim" Alex continued.

"Do not worry, my friend. In this magical ocean, everybody can swim and breathe underneath the water."

"Can we breathe water?!" Alex asked.

"Try and let us know" Khalifa answered.

"Take my hand, daddy. I will take care of you. Khalifa, would you please be a dolphin? Please stay by my dad's side and help him when he needs you."

Khalifa jumped in the water and rays of light engulfed his little fluffy body. He started to swim in circles, and he jumped out of the ocean, as a cute dolphin. His head and body were covered with armour made of gold and precious stones.

"Hey, everybody. Do you want to know why I chose my Khalifa to be a dolphin? My mom said that dolphins have social skills. They rescued drowning sailors by holding them up near the surface to breathe and pushing them to shore. They saved so many people that were too adventurous swimming in the oceans and getting close to drowning. Some dolphins were seen pushing floating objects around the ocean. They collect the treasure chests from the oceans and bring them to the mermaids. Right, Lira? Did you know that dolphin mothers often babysit their calves for up to two years, until they are able to survive on their own? I didn't know that either. My mom told me" Victor said with pride in his voice.

"Thank you, Victor, for the introduction. You are right in everything you said. Jump in the water already. The water is so warm." said Khalifa.

"Wait. I am coming with you, Victor!" said his mom jumping in the water.

"Victor, please wait for us!" said three boys in unison.

Victor looked in their direction and has seen his friends from school: Octavian, Laurentiu and Luca.

"Hey, my friends. You came right on time. Do you want to come with us to visit the underseas civilizations?"

"Of course. Happy Birthday!" they said. "Let's go."

"Thank you, my friends. I am so happy to see you here," said Victor.

Alex, Victor's father, jumped hesitantly in the water holding hands with Victor. He was scared. Victor felt his father was being cautious and said:

"Just stay with me and you will be alright. I promise. Let's swim."

Sanda just looked at Victor and smiled.

Khalifa was holding Alex's body on his back. They started to swim, and, in a few seconds, Alex said:

"I can't breathe. I need air."

"Daddy, you breathe water, and you can talk in this ocean."

"Yes, I can" Alex said with excitement. "I cannot believe it. Yay!!"

Ella looked at everybody getting ready to jump in the ocean and said:

"Before you will all start the journey into this amazing realm, we all must send love vibes and thanks to the oceans. The water is alive. She needs love and thanks, like all of us, in our realm and yours. The ocean will open the real splendor for you to enjoy"

Everybody gave thanks to the waters. They could see that the waters were sparkling in unbelievable beautiful colours.

All children asked their animals to change into different kind of fish: whales, dolphins, sea horses, giant sting rays, and colorful little fish.

Laughing and eager to see the new world, they all jumped in the ocean with more excitement than fear.

"I have a question, please" Victor said. "I know that the water is darker and colder as we will dive deeper in the ocean. Can you tell us how we will see there and how we will be protected from cold water? I have seen on TV that the divers have special costumes and powerful flashlights."

"Do not worry, my dear friend," said Khalifa. "In this magical realm, your body adjust to the pressure and water temperature. You will not feel cold; in fact, you will feel it quite pleasant. Also, your vision will be enhanced thousands of times. You will see the mysterious world in its splendor."

"Thank you so much, Khalifa."

"I want to be a mermaid, Ioana said. Mom, may I, please?"

Dana looked at her and smiling said:

"You can be whoever you want to be. You know what? I will be a mermaid too!"

As they spoke, beautiful tails replaced their legs. Both had dark hair filled with rubies and diamonds. They were happy and started to swim with the yellow and blue fish.

As they all jumped in the ocean and adjusted to the new world, a bright light has seen coming towards them. They were all looking in that direction wondering which surprize they will have.

"What's this?" Victor asked Khalifa.

"Just be patient and you will see" answered Khalifa.

A giant crystal submarine started to get contour as it came closer and closer. The bright light was emanated from the exterior walls, illuminating miles of the ocean. The iridescent light was brighter than the sun light as they knew it from their world, and yet remain comforting for the eyes.

On top of the submarine there it was written "NAUTILUS" in bright flashing lights.

They all looked amazed by this magnificent appearance.

Through the crystal wall they could see somebody waving to them. *Who could it be?* They were wondering.

The front wall of the submarine opened, and Nick was standing there wearing a pilot costume. In his real life he was an illustrious pilot. His son, Liviu, was standing beside him, looking at the people. He knew only a few and he was wondering about the rest of the group.

"Hello, hello! I am Nick and this is my son, Liviu. We will be the pilots on Nautilus today. We will offer you the journey of your life. We came here today to honor Victor's birthday. We are friends with him and his parents."

"Happy birthday!! Victor. May all your wishes come true!" Liviu said. "I am so happy to be here today. We got the approval from Mighty Council of the Magic Wonderland to drive the submarine today."

"Thank you, Liviu. I am so happy that you and your father are here today. It wouldn't be the same without you. We used to play together all the time. But I see that you breathe water too. Isn't there air in the submarine?"

"What's the point?" Nick asked. "We all can breathe water in this realm. In this way, we do not feel the difference of the pressure when we open the walls for the passengers."

"So, we all can come in your submarine during our journey in the oceans?" Victor asked.

"You all are more than welcome, if you all desire" Nick continued. "You will see everything from inside the crystal walls. Nothing is hidden. But you have another choice. You can swim and enjoy the magic of the waters."

"Why is your submarine called "Nautilus"?" Victor said. "I have read the Jules Verne's "Twenty Thousand Leagues Under the Sea" and there was a submarine called like this."

"My dear, this is THE "Nautilus" from the Jules Verne's book. As a child, I always wanted to drive it, and now here is my chance." said Nick.

"As you can see, the books are not always fiction. They look like fiction because people cannot comprehend the evolution or the reality. So, yes, it was a true story, and "Nautilus" was made in this realm almost two millennia ago. Jules Verne was one of the frequent visitors to this world. He was loved by Aqualand people and invited often. Jules borrowed Nautilus to go in the deep waters and to discover its secrets.

Unfortunately, not all visitors in this realm have the chance to see the splendor of this magnificent machine. You know the rule in this magic world. "You have to believe in order to see". If you see it and you do not believe it, it's like you do not see it at all. They consider it as a fruit of their imagination and do not believe it's real. Ha, ha, ha, ha, I haven't had so much fun in a long time." Nick continued.

"So, who is coming on board? Do not be afraid" Nick said. "We have room for everybody."

"What can you tell us about the submarine? Where is this bright light coming from, through the walls? It's all around" Victor said.

"The light comes from the power of the crystal. This is a magical crystal that is found only on the bottom of the oceans and is guarded by the mighty army lead by Toto, the Count of Crystal Land", continued Nick.

"This submarine is 70 metres long, capable of sinking any ship, and equipped with a 12,000-volume library and an art collection with works by Leonardo Da Vinci, Titian, and Raphael. I hope you will all come and visit it. It's just a unique piece of art that not everybody will have the chance to see. The art collection, the riches of this submarine are priceless."

"Wow, I remember this; I've read it in the book. Dad, mom, can we go inside?" Victor asked his parents.

"For sure, and Khalifa can come with us too. Will you all come with us?" Sanda asked her family and friends.

"Yes, yes" they all said in unison.

"I will not miss it for the world!" Khalifa said laughing.

Everybody was boarding the submarine and they were all in awe. The riches inside were unimaginable, indescribable.

"Here is a splendor of gold furniture, gold chairs and tables with priceless gems, transparent gold plates and silverware that were not described in the book. Also, we all breathe water here and there are thousands of books and unique artworks done by Leonardo Da Vinci, Titian, and Rafael. How are they preserved? I didn't see them when we were little. Gabriela, do you remember them?" Sanda asked.

"No, they were not here" Gabriela answered.

"Let me answer to your question" Lira said. As you already know, the dolphins collect the precious items from the bottom of the oceans, and they bring them to us. We preserve them as per old Aqualand's technology. All books, paintings, statues, in fact all unique values and riches found at the bottom of the oceans are covered with an invisible layer of the purest air. You can read a book under the water, and nothing will damage the book. Every page has all around a thin layer of the purest air. The gold and all very rare gems are not affected by water. We decided to place a few here. We have many treasure chests in our hidden locations. You see, this submarine is always protected by the most powerful Aqualand's' army."

"Wow, even Jules Verne would be impressed" Sanda said.

"The leader of our army is your friend Tudor. In our world, he is Toto, The Count of Crystal Land, Protector of Visible and Invisible Realms, Keeper of the Treasures in Known and Unknown Worlds. He decided to live in this magic world. We know that he dedicated his life in protecting people in need, and he is so good at that. We watched him during his work on Earth and we were all very impressed."

"Oh, Tudor? Where is he? We would like to see him" Sanda exclaimed.

"He is now preparing the defence for our journey." Lira continued.

"Defence? Are we in danger?"

"No, dear. Do not fear. But there are a few humans that will never give up in looking for Aqualand. Tudor developed a very funny and effective system against them. He applied the earth rules to the oceans, and they work. You will see him soon. For sure we will have these encounters along the way, and we try to keep them as far as possible from our world."

"This is Tudor all right. He is so funny and when he loves something, nothing stays in his way to protect it. We know him for a long time. He is one of our dearest friends" said Sanda with a big smile on her face.

TOTO, COUNT OF CRYSTAL LAND, GREAT PROTECTOR OF VISIBLE AND INVISIBLE REALMS, KEEPER OF THE TRESURES IN KNOWN AND UNKNOWN WORLDS AND HIS MIGHTY ARMY

There was a silent moment when they all were looking outside the walls and processing the information they just heard. That was the moment when they realized that Nautilus was escorted by whales, sea hoses, sharks, dolphins, and monster fish they didn't know. They were all around the submarine. As strange as it looked for them, they all had armours covering their bodies from head to tail. The armours were made of gold.

A Kraken, the largest sea monster ever imagined, appeared in front of the submarine.

"Mom, what's this?" Victor asked.

"It's a Kraken, my dear."

"Kraken?"

"Yes, it is the largest known sea monster. But do not be afraid, my dear. Look closely. There is somebody on his head" Sanda said.

"Who is that?" Victor asked.

"Hello, hello, Victor. Happy birthday to you and your cousin!!"Toto said from Kraken's head.

"Thank you, Toto! So nice to see you here. This is a nice surprise. What are you riding?" Victor asked.

"As your mom said, it is a Kraken, the biggest sea monster. Do not be afraid of these giant tentacles; this monster rarely attacks humans, preferring to stay in deep waters where he eats only huge quantities of fish" Toto continues. "Because of his huge size, people fear him and run or sail away... ha, ha, ha, ha... I chose him as my ride because of his enormous tentacles that when he claps them together, a signal is sent to all living creatures in the oceans; he warns them of the intruders. Each fish or monster come together to protect our realm. We avoid wars as much as we can, but if they are unavoidable, we do not step back."

"I like your outfit" Victor said. "Do you have this shimmering costume because you are a Count of Crystal Land? What is Crystal Land?" Victor asked. "I never heard about it."

117

"No, dear. I have this outfit as a Great Protector of Visible and Invisible Realms. I have different outfits for different responsibilities. Crystal Land is an underwater glamorous city that is protected by many glowing moving crystals."

"Wow, your costume must be expensive!" Victor exclaimed.

"Not at all. Just think of it and it's done. Simple like that" Toto said. "Do not forget that we are in a magical world."

Toto had a tight-fitting gold diving costume with a belt made of white sapphires. His golden boots were covered also in the same precious gemstones. In his hand he had a gold trident.

"And the trident? Is this yours?" Victor asked looking at the magnificent gold trident.

"Yes, it is mine, and is made from a part of Poseidon's Trident. Did you hear about it?" Toto continued.

"No. I didn't. Is it something special about it?" Victor asked.

"Yes, it is. Poseidon was the God of Seas, and his Trident contains within it an intense magical energy. Poseidon's Trident had the power over the seas; it made tsunamis and waves and could calm the water or make it roar. If Poseidon strikes the Earth with his trident, a catastrophic earthquake will happen.

My Trident is very powerful too. I can summon my Kraken or any other sea creature, I can make waves and huge waterfalls inside the oceans, and I can heal any hurt sea animal by simply touching it with the trident. In this realm, I can control the same powers that Poseidon had."

"Waterfalls inside the ocean? Will we see them today?" Victor kept asking. His thirst for knowledge was pure and infinite.

"In fact, you will see them quite soon. Aqualand's entrance is protected by a huge waterfall, not only by an invisible shield. In front of the waterfall, there is the Crystal Land. I created it. There are colorful glowing crystals rising from the bottom of the ocean. The crystals are in a continuous movement; they change positions, their patterns, and colours. The view is spectacular. The intruders believe that they found a treasure and when they want to take crystals with them, the crystals just disappear from their hands and go back in a different place and in a different position. Some tried to take pictures of the Crystal Land, but they couldn't. The crystals are invisible in the pictures. When they see that, they run as fast as they can, believing that they are in a ghost location of the ocean. Ha-ha-ha... it's so easy to fool them... ha, ha, ha.

Very few reach this area in the ocean. Usually, we stop them way before they are here" Toto continued.

"How?" Victor asked.

LET'S HAVE SOME FUN!

Toto didn't have a chance to answer right away. A wave of vibrations sent by Kraken was felt in the water. Everybody looked around to see what happened as they all felt it. The fish army started to move fast in an attack position surrounding the submarine.

"Nick, place the invisible shield for the submarine. Now!" Toto said.

"Not again" Nick said. He pushed a button. The walls closed and the submarine was invisible.

"What happened?" Sanda asked. "This is new for me."

"Intruders happened. They are invisible for us, but my army can see them through their vigilant eyes." Toto answered.

"Let's have some fun! Victor, now I will answer your question. Just watch" Toto continued with excitement in his voice.

He touched once the bottom of the ocean with his trident. The shield that protected the intruders' small submarine disappeared. Toto touched again the bottom of the ocean with his trident. A traffic sign appeared in front of the intruders: "Speed limit 5 km".

Everybody could see the intruders' faces when they saw the sign. With confusion, the unwanted visitors hit the brakes. They started to move very slowly looking around for any other signs.

Again, Toto touched the bottom of the ocean. Many highway roads appeared in front of the visitors. "Aqualand" signs with arrows in different directions were on all of them.

The intruders' confusion grew. They didn't know which highway to choose, until one sign started flashing. They were seen moving slowly towards that highway.

"I would like to hear what they are talking about right now" Victor said. "For sure it's hilarious."

Nick pushed another button, and everybody could hear the intruders talking in a speaker.

"What's this? How come there are highways in the oceans?" asked one intruder.

"The people from Aqualand are very advanced civilization. For sure they built them" said the other one. "Let's follow the signs. I am sure we are very close."

"It must be new. Nobody ever reported these highways" said the first intruder.

"Nobody was ever so close to Aqualand" the other one responded. *"But here we are, and we will make history! I can't wait to see it and take with us as many of the riches as we can find. For sure they are worth lots of money. We will be so rich and famous."*

Toto touched again the ocean sand with his trident. This time he changed the mindset of the unwanted visitors. He made them believe that they were on the highway for at least a few hours. Another sign could be seen: "Aqualand - Next Two Exits".

"I knew we are on the right track. Just follow the signs and keep the speed limit."

"Why do they need a speed limit in the ocean?"

"I do not know. We will find out soon. I will take pictures of what we see here so we can show them to the world."

Toto created the same illusion of passing time and distance and another sign was seen: "Aqualand - 1 ¾ Exit", and the highway turned smooth in a 90-degree angle to the right.

"What means "1 ¾ exit"?"

"Maybe there are other cities in the oceans where their civilizations disappeared long ago. We go for Aqualand only and we will not stop for anything else."

"Just take pictures of this sign. Nobody will believe us."

The intruders kept driving their small submarine and soon they could see another sign:" Aqualand Next Exit"

"I told you we are close. Keep following the signs and soon we will be rich."

Again, the highway had a smooth turn of 90 degrees to the right. The intruders didn't realize that they were going back in the direction they came from.

All people from Nautilus were looking to see what will happen next. The unwanted visitors kept driving slowly, respecting the speed limit.

Again, Toto touched the bottom of the ocean with his trident and created the illusion of time and space passing.

When there was enough distance in between Nautilus and the intruders, Toto laughed and touched again the sand with his magic trident.

All the sudden, the highway disappeared. The intruders were kept in a pitch-dark water.

"What did you do? I told you to keep the highway. Where is it?"

"I didn't do anything. I don't know what happened. I am so confused. It was here a moment ago."

"No worries, it must be a trick of the Aqualand civilization. But we are smart. Keep going in the same direction and we will find it without any signs."

They kept driving in the dark water and disappear in the abyss.

Victor and his friends kept looking at them until they were lost in the depth of the dark waters.

"And this is how is done!" said Toto laughing hard.

They all started to laugh.

"This is genius!" Victor said. "What if they came with guns and started to shoot at us?"

"This would be impossible" Toto said. Nobody can see what you all see until we allow it. Nobody can see Nautilus; they do not expect to see it in the oceans, and they don't. We want to keep peace in between land and water civilizations. But if we must fight, we will not be defeated. We are the most powerful army in the world, as well as magic of the realm on our side."

AQUALAND

As Nautilus was diving deeper and deeper in the waters, a fascinating world was revealed to them. Brighter and brighter waters were all around. The light was brighter than the Sun light, as they know it, but very comfortable to the eyes.

The Crystal Land was glowing with iridescent colours. The crystals were moving graciously as if they were dancing and kissing each other in a soundless magical music. Toto strikes his magic trident. The crystals were alive and bowed to him, immersing deep in the ocean golden sand. A wonderful city rouses from the depths of the ocean floor. Crystal buildings decorated in red, white, and black stones, illuminated by the bright light that irradiated from inside the walls, made the view a splendor for the eye. Mermaids and fish were swimming happily together.

A little further, a huge waterfall replaced the crystals. Looking at Victor, Toto winked mischievously and whistle beautifully towards the waterfall. The waterfall responded with the same whistle and separated into two huge falls. They started to glide aside like curtains on a stage, revealing the bright rainbow shield.

"I am the Count of Crystal Land, Great Protector of Visible and Invisible Realms, Keeper of the Treasures in Known and Unknown Worlds!" Toto said with a strong laud voice. "Please open the gates, Mighty Council of Aqualand. Today we have visitors from the world above. Here is a Golden Boy with his family and friends."

Gently, he touched the shield with his trident.

The rainbow shield dissolved in millions and millions of colourful butterflies, which disappeared in the ocean like fireworks. The scenery was spectacular; it could be seen by everybody. The beauty and the dance of the lights were indescribable.

A new world revealed itself.

Bright sparkling forest trees were covering the bottom of the oceans. Amazing flowers, unseen on Earth before, with iridescent colours, were sending rainbow lights all around. Every petal was rich and heavy in priceless gems. The ocean grass was covered with glowing rich stones.

Fish, all sizes and forms, with electrical rays were hiding in the magnificent vegetation. They raised their heads above the plants just to say "Hi!" to the visitors and then rapidly hid underneath the spectacular flowers and seaweeds.

Beautiful temples and palaces made of crystal, gold, and silver, and covered with brilliant colourful precious stones, were everywhere. The roads were paved in gold.

Golden flying machines looked so busy flying quietly above the magnificent architectural buildings.

The view was magnificent, and the visitors were looking in wonder.

"Mom, it's so beautiful" Victor said." It was the same here when you were a little girl?"

"Oh, yes, it was. I remember when we came here for the first time. I couldn't believe my eyes. I couldn't even imagine such a beautiful world" Sanda said.

"So, you came here many times?" Victor asked.

"Many, many times, my dear. Gabriela and I had so much fun" Sanda continued.

"It's so true" Gabriela said. "Now is your time to discover the unknown and to see the world of all possibilities and riches. There is more to be seen and to be bewildered about. Just enjoy."

"While we will visit this world, I would like to tell you the real story of Aqualand" Ada said.

"Please do. We are all eager to hear it" Victor said, having one arm around Khalifa.

Ada continued:

"Aqualand is described as a mythical island with a mythical civilization. There lives a powerful and advanced kingdom.

There are many legends related to Aqualand. Plato, the Greek philosopher, described Aqualand as an island located in the Atlantic Ocean. The island was protected by the sea gods, who made Aqualas king, and named the island by his name. The Aqualand grew powerful, being the only civilization that possessed a very advance technology.

Fortunately, to this very day, the mystery of Aqualand remains unfolded to humans. The passion of humanity for knowledge never seized, and the humans think that the answer to this long-debated civilization will surface soon. I can assure you that this is not possible unless we will decide to unfold the truth. Its location is protected by all of us in this realm."

Khalifa continued the story:

> "There is another legend which is similar to the first one and describes Aqualand' birth in detail, stating that the Aqualand city was built by Poseidon, the God of the Seas. Poseidon walked through the world to find an island for himself. The one he chose was inhabited by half-god and half-human beings. He fell in love with a woman named Kuanda when he saw her first time on this island. He built a home for his love in the City of Aqualand, on top of a hill. The island was isolated in the ocean.

> The legend says that the Aqualandeans lived for at least eight hundred years. They were farmers, grew their own food with the help of a well-maintained irrigation system and animals. They had access to rare metals and used crystals extensively for relaxation. They built beautiful buildings and statues, all plated in gold and priceless gems."

"These are legends. What is the real story?" Victor asked. "I am sure you know the real one, not only the myths and legends."

"Our story, as Aqualandeans, is more advanced and simpler than anybody can guess" Lira said. "So here it goes: Aqualand is our land from the beginning of time. We are all gods. We know all the secrets of the earth, water, space, and we master magic. We all have incommensurable powers over all known and unknown elements in the universe, and on our planet's surface. We can control the weather, volcanic eruption, ocean waves and storms. We can easily channel valuable energy from time and space.

Aqualand always has been in this realm. It will always be. We are immortal. We are the civilization that had developed planes, submarines, X-ray machines, flying machines, anti-gravity devices, and crystals that control energy from the sun; we made them all from the beginning of time. We built the pyramids in Egypt and America, and we have strong connections with civilizations from another universe.

During our eons of life, there were a few explores who were granted passage into our world. We love humans so much, and we wanted to share our knowledge with all mankind. Unfortunately, most of them had only searched for our land for the purpose of accumulating as much treasure as they could.

To ensure they will not reveal the location of Aqualand, we created the legends and planted them in their minds. Of course, when they went back in your world, they started to spread the word. This is how Plato wrote his book; he heard the story from somebody, and that somebody from somebody else, and this is how story goes for nine thousand years, earth time. And because nobody can say exactly where Aqualand is located, they keep trying to find it to this day. "Lira continued.

"Aqualand is everywhere, like everything else in this Magic Wonderland. You must believe to see it. Nobody destroyed Aqualand, nobody could. We are here and we will always be." said Ella.

"There were a few scientists that could come in our world and there were new technologies that were so helpful for humans' evolution. Through these new advanced technologies, sometimes we have intruders in the oceans, close to our world. The Aqualand is surrounded by an invisible shield, and they cannot invade our world. They want only monetary gain and riches. We want to teach humankind as much as we can, but they are so limited to the material world.

Only pure heart people are allowed now in this realm, and we know that they will not tell a soul about us. That's why you are here, you are the chosen ones, and we trust you." Lira said.

"Did you have other chosen ones in Aqualand?" Victor asked.

"Of course. There are so many pure and innocent people on Earth. We love them all and they in reverse protect our location."

"Will you ever reveal your realm to the world?" Victor asked eager to hear more.

"Yes, we will, when the right time will come. All civilizations from the oceans and inner core, all mythic animals that you see here, all plants and mountains, all riches will be seen by everybody. We watch all people, and we maintain the balance in your world."

"Balance? What kind of balance?" Victor asked.

"Balance in between good and bad forces in the universe, which affect our earth too. People are good by nature, but bad things happen to them. We are all here to protect them and we will rise to protect the humankind."

"Did you have many intruders in Aqualand City before?" Paul asked.

"Yes, dear, we had."

"How come? I thought you have the strongest security to protect the planet. Plus, you are surrounded by an invisible shield."

"Yes, dear, we are, but sometimes we let it down. There are advanced ships created by humans that are invisible to the naked eye and they reach our world. If they are not welcome, Toto comes in place with his army and diverts them in a very easy and funny way. We all laugh about it. Sometimes we wonder why we didn't do it from the beginning."

"Divert? The way that he just did?" Paul said. "I can't stop laughing... ha, ha, ha"

"Yes, my dear. It was so funny. The intruders come here all the time" Ada said.

"So, Aqualand is real, always has been and always will be here. You are eternal; you live to protect my kind, and to make our journey funny. Is this right?" Victor asked mostly as a conclusion.

"That's right, my dear friend" Ada said knowing that Victor will ask more questions. *"Victor is really the chosen one. He wants to know everything, and mostly, he loves everybody"* Ada was thinking. *"This is how he will always be: pure and innocent. We know it."*

ZOE

THE PRINCESS OF AQUALAND

As Nautilus was flowing slowly above the Aqualand, a magnificent building appeared in front of them. A "Wow" was heard in the crowd. All the people in the submarine were left speechless by the beauty and size of the structures. Immense columns made from precious stones were all around the castle. The castle itself was made from crystal decorated in gold and diamonds.

"Can we go inside this castle?" Victor asked.

"We will all go inside to thank Princess Zoe for letting us inside her realm" Toto said.

When they all stepped inside the magnificent building, they saw three royal thrones in the middle of a huge room. The beauty and the riches of that room left them all speechless. Huge gold statues of gods with their horses and chariots were all around the throne. They saw a girl about Victor's age sitting graciously on a magnificent throne. She was wearing a white dress with diamonds everywhere, a gold cape and a gold little crown.

They all bowed in front of the Princess and Victor said:

> "We are all honoured to visit your world and we want to thank you for allowing us to come here. We are amazed of the beauty of your rich realm. I have never seen something like this before. I couldn't even imagine" he continued with excitement.

> "I am honoured to meet you all" said Princess Zoe, "and I am happy that I can wish you and your cousin "Happy Birthday". I am Princess Zoe, Princess of Aqualand. As you can see, I am just a little girl. I am the last descendant of Aqualas, the first Aqualandean King."

Graciously she showed her parents, the King, and the Queen, with her little hands and continued:

> "The blood of Aqualas runs through my father's veins, King Andrew, and mine. My mother, Queen Jessica, is a descendant of Aphrodite, the Goddess of Love and Beauty. My parents are immortal and so am I. And here is my playful dog, Xena. She is my best friend. We play every day."

Xena heard her name, looked at the princess and then happy wiggled her tail.

The King and the Queen looked at their precious Princess and whispered something in her ears. She looked happy for what she heard.

> "My parents just granted me the honor to welcome you and to answer any question you might have"

Princess Zoe said. "You are more than welcome to explore my realm. My people are always happy to have pure hearted humans in our world. Everything you all see here is revealed to you with much confidence. All the buildings and high advanced technology were created by my ancestors, and still more is created."

"Thank you so much for your kindness, Your Majesty" Victor said. "Mom said that we will go for a treasure hunt, just for fun."

"I would like to accompany you, but I am afraid that I will spoil your joy. You see, I know all treasure locations. Sometimes I am going there with Xena and play."

"Before we will go for hunt, can we ask you a few questions?" Victor asked curiously.

"Of course. My parents gave me permission to answer any questions you may have."

"Can you tell us how you spend a day?" Victor asked.

"In our world, there is no day or night. The time stays still, like in the Magic Wonderland. We are never tired, and we have so many things to do. I am learning wisdom from the ancient gods, and I am discovering how to control my magic powers and my mind in the benefit of the whole world. I observe how the new advanced technology is made and I learn how to use it. Everything is so interesting, and I am always eager to learn more. I am like you, Victor. We were born with the same thirst for knowledge and wisdom. That's why my parents allowed you all to come here.

We have an enormous flowers garden in the back of the castle. The flowers are so beautiful, they are breathless. Also, they have healing powers.

Xena is with me everywhere I go. She loves to protect me. Sometimes I asked for her advice, and she is always willing to teach me secrets of the unknown. She is like Khalifa, the King of Small Animals' Realm, and your companion. By the way, I do not see him. He didn't come with you?"

"I am right here, Your Highness. I am a cute dolphin now, ha, ha, ha … as Victor requested. Thank you for taking time to be with us" Khalifa said. "I believe you remember when I came here a few times to play with you and Xena. Magical times…" said Khalifa with melancholy in his voice.

"Of course, I remember. We played together and we had so much fun. Your teachings are so precious to me. Now is time to teach Victor. Your wisdom will guide him through his life."

"That's why I am thinking to pass the crown to another small animal from our realm and to spend all my time with Victor" Khalifa answered.

"Wise move, my friend," said Princess Zoe.

"I have a question, said Mihai. We have names like Zoe, Andrew, and Jessica in our world. I thought that the King and the Queen of Aqualand would have more sophisticated names."

"My parents decided to take human names in honor of humankind, which they love so much. We all love our names. They may be common in your world, but they are unique in ours" Princess Zoe answered.

"One question, please," said Paul. "Do you know how to fly a flying machine? You have so many here. People say that sometimes they are seen on earth too. They say that these are Unidentified Flying Objects from outer space."

"Yes, I know how to fly them. Here, all children are taught how to fly the flying machines. The flying saucers that are seen in your world could be ours or not. Sometimes we go in your world to observe and to protect. Sometimes the civilizations from the universe come on Earth to protect the humankind. We are friends with them, and we are always in contact. We learned from them new technologies that are way advanced to be given to people on earth. We save them here and will be given to humankind when the right time will come

"When will be right time?" Paul asked. "Ada said the same thing."

"Nobody knows when, but we all know that it will come, and we will be ready to reveal ourselves in order to protect the world."

"What do you eat mostly?" Paul asked.

"We eat algae, seaweeds, some very nutritious sea plants found deep in the sea forests."

"No fish?" Paul asked curiously.

"No fish. They are our friends. We play with them, and they are our protectors too" Princess Zoe answered.

"We would like to spend more time with you, dear Princess, but off we go now to continue our journey" Khalifa said. "We thank you again for everything you shared with us. Be sure that nothing will be disclosed in human's world."

"We know that. Enjoy the rest of your journey. I am sure it will be very pleasant" Princess Zoe said. "We will miss you all and we hope you will come again."

They all bowed as they exited the castle. They were all so impressed about everything and were so quiet.

TREASURE HUNT
IN AQUALAND

"Thank you, Toto, for bringing us here" Sanda said. "We are all speechless. It's even more beautiful than I remember."

"So, what's next? Will we all go on treasure hunt?" asked Victor.

"Only the children with their animals, my army and me. Do not forget that I am the Protector of Treasures in Known and Unknown Worlds. Here is always the Unknown World and I want to protect the children," said Toto.

"Children, do you want to find a treasure in these oceans?" Toto asked knowing the answer.

"Yes, yes, yes" they all answered very happy.

"Why don't you look for the treasures in my castle?" Princess Zoe said. "I am sure the King and the Queen will allow you to do this."

"Do you have treasure chests in the castle, beside all riches all around?" Victor asked.

"Of course, we have. My land is very rich; people above cannot imagine how rich we are. No king or emperor was ever as rich as we are. I am sure you were told that everything will be given to the people when the right time will come."

"Dear Count of Crystal Land, Protector of Visible and Invisible Realms, Keeper of the Treasures in Known and Unknown Worlds, we appreciate that you want to keep the children safe, but they are safe in my castle. There are no monsters inside. Just let them enjoy."

"Yes, Your Majesty" said Toto and bowed.

"I have some riddles from my teachers. Would you like to hear them?" Princess Zoe asked the children.

"Yes, please" they answered.

"Here is the first riddle that you must pass in order to go on a treasure hunt" Princess Zoe said. *"If you have one, you want to share it. But once you share it, you do not have it. What is it?"*

"Hmmm" Victor said. "What could it be?"

"I know, I know. It's a banana, or an apple, or a hotdog" Andy said.

"Oh, dear brother, you are thinking about food all the time" Paul told to Andy.

"I am hungry" Andy said. "I would love to eat some seaweeds or algae. I am sure they are so good."

A gold plate full of algae and seaweeds appeared in his hands. He started to eat and was very pleased with the delicious taste.

"It cannot be food" Victor said. "I don't believe they have the bananas or apples here."

"What is then? What do we want to share?" Andy said.

"We share everything, we are brothers" Paul said. "But again, is not food."

"So, I have something that I want to share, and when I share, I don't have it…" Victor was thinking out loud. "I can share with you all my toys, but this is not the answer. Must be something more meaningful, like a thought. Yes, I know."

"It's a secret!!!" All children said at the same time, and they started to laugh.

"It was easy. I knew it from the beginning" Andy said with pride in his voice continuing to eat.

"Well done!" Princess Zoe said. "I am happy you found the right answer. So, you know that what we share with you is a secret."

"We can keep a secret. We promise" children said.

"Now is the second riddle that will guide you to the treasure: *"I have keys but no locks and feet but no socks. What am I?"* Princess Zoe read from a very old parchment.

"I know this, I play it every day" Victor said. "It's my piano."

"Very good Victor, but I believe is my piano" Princess said laughing.

"Do you have a piano? Do you play piano?" Victor asked with admiration.

"Yes, of course, and I love it. When I play piano, the music is heard in my realm. The fish come to my castle to listen closer."

"Where is your piano?" Paul asked.

"Just look all around this large room and you will see it" Princess said.

The children looked around and they saw the piano in the further corner of the room.

"Before you go there, I must read for you the last riddle" Princess Zoe said.

"Look inside me and you will see
A candle, a lamp, a button, and a bee
Touch me once, don't be afraid
I won't bite, I'll fly instead"

"Let's go to the piano" Victor said. *'Look inside me'* We must lift the lid."

The children ran to the piano and lifted the lid, as per riddle. Inside there were a candle, a bright luminous lamp, a button, and a bee flying happy.

"Dad, I found your coat button. It's here" Lorand said to his father with excitement.

"I cannot believe it. I was looking for it whole week. How is this possible?" Mickey asked.

"You lost it last week while you were walking with Gabriela and your children by the lake shore. You bended over the water to see your reflection and the button just dropped. The dolphins found it and brought it here. We knew you will be here today, and we saved it for you" Princess said.

"Thank you so much, Your Highness. This coat is very precious to me. I got it from my wife for my birthday."

The children surrounded the piano and started to touch everything.

"Do not do that" Victor said. "The candle, the lamp and the buttons do not fly. Only the bee flies, but first we must catch it; she is flying all around inside the piano."

"It is a magic world. Everything is possible, even the impossible" Paul said.

"Yes, it's true. But the riddle says:

'*Touch me once, don't be afraid*
I won't bite, I'll fly instead'.

My mom told me that the bees can be caught easily if they are left undisturbed. They sting if they are provoked" Victor said. "Let's wait for the bee to sit somewhere and we will touch it afterwards. She will not feel threatened and will not sting us."

"Ok, ok" children said, waiting patiently for the bee to sit somewhere.

They were waiting quietly, and the bee stopped flying. She was sitting on the button, quietly surrounding her body with her little wings. She looked like she was falling asleep. The children were waiting for a sign that she will fly again, but she was quietly resting on Mickey's button.

"Victor, please let me touch the bee. I am not afraid" Lorand said whispering.

"Of course. Please do."

Lorand touched gently the bee's wings. The bee opened her little eyes, had a naughty look, and started to fly above the children and then started to whistle a beautiful melody. The children started to laugh; they didn't expect that.

The bee began to take little brown dots from her little invisible pockets, and she threw them all around. These dots started in an instant to grow bigger and bigger. Beautiful treasure chests appeared in front of them. There were so many, all around the gigantic room.

"Mom, it's amazing!" Victor said. "Can we open one to see inside?"

"Of course, my dear."

The kids easily opened one chest and when they saw what's inside, they all said "Wow". Gold coins, huge precious stones, gold tiaras and crowns heavy with diamonds delighted their eyes.

"Can we touch them?" Lorand asked.

"Of course, touch them. Try a crown if you want" Princess Zoe replied.

Lorand put a crown on his cute head and said:

"Mom, I am a Prince now."

"You are always my little prince, with or without a crown" Gabriel said smiling.

"I do not understand something" Paul said. "How is it possible that this little bee has invisible pockets full of huge chests?"

"Magic. Just basic magic" Princess Zoe said. "We have so many bees that protect our treasures and we don't want the treasures to be exposed. We protect the bees as they protect our riches."

"And they all whistle so beautifully?" Paul asked

"Yes, they do. They whistle only when they are happy, and they are always happy to show what they keep in their pockets. They are so cute" the princes said. "This was Toto's idea. He always comes with funny ideas, and we love them."

"Thank you, your Highness. Now I know."

"Thank you again, Your Majesties, for your kindness and for making this journey very exciting for children," said Khalifa. "Now we must go. New adventures are waiting for us."

"It was our pleasure, dear friend," said the Princess. "We hope you will all be back soon. You will always be welcomed here."

They all bowed and left the castle to continue their exciting adventures!

GOLD CITY

"Mom, it is so beautiful in Aqualand. I would love to come back here to learn more about their civilization" Victor said.

"For sure you will come back. This is your destiny, my dear: to learn more and more about these magic worlds. You are a part of them now, and they are part of you. Khalifa will be with you all the time."

"I will teach Victor everything I thought you and Gabriela" Khalifa said to Sanda. "I will show him everything in your world and this magic world. Victor will see in time that both worlds are filled with wonder and magic."

"Where are we going now?" Victor asked.

"Let's ask Ada if we can go and visit Gold City" Khalifa said. "Gold City is a hidden world beneath the surface of the planet, and only the pure hearted humans can visit it."

"My dear friends, it is not easy to enter Gold City, and the reason is that Gold City exist in our pure hearts" Ada answered. "This is a real place. The open pure heart is the only way to Gold City. The fastest way to Gold City is LOVE. Infinite love is the only truth and the only way to Gold City. Everything else is an illusion."

"There is an old Tibetan story about a young man who was in search for Gold City." continued Ada. "After crossing many high mountains, he arrived at a cave of an old hermit, who asked him:

"Where are you going across these wastes of snow?"

"To find Gold City," the youth replied.

"Ah, well then, you need not travel far," the hermit said. *"The kingdom of Gold City is in your own heart."*

The young man continued traveling far in the highest mountains; he endures the cold and the hunger, until he truly believed that Gold City exists. His heart opened, and true magic embraced him in an instant. He took a deep breath and a magnificent new world opened in front of his eyes. The new reality looked like a dream, where ordinary space and time physics no longer applied. He was in awe. The new world revealed in front of his eyes was surreal."

"Is this true?" Victor asked.

"Of course, it is true," Ada said. "My friend here, Khalifa, was the hermit. He can confirm that."

"It is true, my dear friends. I can take many forms and I can guide everyone to their own destination. Humans fear what they do not understand or what they do not see. Believe when I say that everyone is a force for good. Everybody is looking for the best inside them or in others." said Khalifa.

"Which is the fastest way to reach Gold City?" Toto asked. "I believe we need the approval from the Master of the World, which is the ruler of the underground world. All my friends here want to spend some time today in the Red Realm. I know that time stands still in this realm, but on the surface is late afternoon."

"I am happy to say that the Master of the World has granted Victor's wish to visit Gold City together with his friends and family" Ada answered. "The fastest way is to touch the ocean ground with your Trident, speed up the time and transport everybody at the holy place."

"Mom, dad, we go to visit Gold City" Aden said with excitement in his voice. "Can we guide them in our world?"

Chodrak, his father said:

"Of course, we can, if this honor is given to us by Matiar and Mariat."

"Who is Matiar and Mariat?" Victor asked very curious.

"They are the two entities that assist the Master of the World in his infinite wisdom. Matiar knows the purposes of future events, and Mariat rules the causes of those events. The Master of the Worlds knows all the forces of the world, reads all the souls of mankind, and writes the great book of their destiny."

"Wow, does he know the destiny of all of us?" Victor asked.

"Of course," said Chodrak. "He is the perfect immortal being and his knowledge is infinite."

Toto turned to his best friend, the Kraken, and said:

"My dear friend, I let you in charge of protecting Aqualand. You are the leader of my army until I will be back. Follow the same rules we've made, and it will be all right. If any security problems arise, send me the message through my Trident. I will be there in an instant. Meanwhile, I will escort the crew to the Gold City."

"Can we come to visit Gold City?" Nick asked. "This will be our only opportunity for the time being. There are very rare occasions when the visitors are accepted in the holy land. The reason I am asking is because we do not have the gold star."

"No worries, Nick. All my friends are invited today to spend time with me and my family.

Khalifa, can we get the gold stars for Nick and Liviu?" asked Victor.

"Let's ask Nemo" said Khalifa looking around to see Nemo.

Nemo just appeared close to Khalifa, with a big smile on his face.

"I heard my name, dear friend. I am at your service" Nemo continued.

"Can we give gold stars to Nick and his son? We would like them to join us in the holy land."

"That is not a problem" Nemo said. He took his right paw, made a circle in the air and the gold stars appeared on Nick's and Liviu's hands.

"Wahoo!" Liviu said. "I have it. I am so happy, dad."

"Me too, my son. Me too."

"Did you get the approval from the Master of the World?" Nemo asked Khalifa.

"Yes, we did! His almighty arranged already for us to have a quick and lovely visit."

"This is so rare, my friend, so rare. Many people asked us to see Gold City, but only a few went there. Enjoy your trip, my friends. My duty calls." said Nemo and off he went.

"Now that we are all here, let's make a nice entrance"
Toto said.

Toto touched the ocean floor and in a blink of the eye, they were all in front of a beautiful gate. Gorgeous carves were all over the wood gate. An ancient lock, with magical functions, was always keeping the gate closed. Only the gate keeper had the power and knowledge to open the gate, and only for pure heart people without any hidden intensions. No humans had or will ever have the power to open these gates. No tools were ever made in the human world that can open it. They tried many times, no wonder, but they all left the gates thinking that they are in the front of an illusion.

Toto raised his hand and knock on the gates. At the same time, a monk opened the doors. He had a big smile on his face. A long light blue robe with a brown belt and roman sandals were his outfit.

"Please come inside" he said. "The Master of the World granted your wish today to visit the forbidden kingdom. Gold City's location and nature remains a subject of disputes in your world, but in this magic world, we all know the exact location and now you are also accepted in our realm. Please do not forget that the main requirement to be a part of this world is to have a pure heart. For sure you must know that all animals and birds have a pure heart."

They all went inside the mythical place. Only few humans had ever seen it. Magnificent pillars of light shot skywards, and glowing stones provided constant light in this realm. The roads were paved with white and red gemstones. The houses were made of the purest crystal with gold plates around the windows and doors. They all stared in wonder.

"Mom, it is so beautiful here, like nothing I have ever seen before in our world" Victor said with admiration.

"The beauty is as unimaginable as their wisdom and knowledge" Sanda said. "Believe me my son, this is the first time I visit this realm, and I am sure this is just because for you and Lorand. You both are special with pure and noble hearts, and I am sure that you will be allowed to visit anytime."

"Chodrak, what can you tell us about your world?" Victor asked Aden' father.

"In Sanskrit, Gold City means *"mighty world "*.

"We are millions of people that live in Gold City. We enjoy perfect happiness and never know suffering; we do not desire any material thing and we do not age.

Our world is a labyrinth of multiple dimensions.

Only the pure of heart can live in Gold City, enjoying perfect happiness, never knowing suffering or old age. Love and wisdom reign and injustice is unknown. We have beautiful, perfect bodies, and possess supernatural powers. Our spiritual knowledge is deep, and our technological level is highly advanced. Our thirst for studying the arts and sciences has no limits, and they are on a far higher level than anything the outside world has attained." said Chodrak.

Monks were walking around them, bowing with respect and serenity. Victor's family and friends bowed and smiled back. No words were spoken. No words were needed.

"What do you eat in this world? Do you harvest crops? Is your water clean?" Lorand asked.

"We irrigate our crops with holy waters and keep them warm with the powerful rays of the *"Great Light"*, which is produced by a secret machine given to us by gods thousands of years ago. We eat what we harvest, and we drink the holy waters."

""*Great Light*" given to you by gods?" Paul asked.

"Yes, by gods. They are still with us but on a higher level of existence.

Our knowledge is hidden in other dimension and is forbidden to common people, until they will understand it and use it for the benefit of mankind. At that time, we will reveal ourselves to mankind and we will teach them everything we know from the beginning of time."

"So, the knowledge is forbidden for us?" Victor asked curiously.

"No, it's not. It is just that our knowledge is far more advanced than you have in your world. The humans are not ready yet to live their life at a higher scientific and wisdom level. The material world dominates all over the human's world. Here, we do not have that eager to accumulate things just to feel more powerful.

We are all equal and all the knowledge is given to us freely. It is the same in all underworld realms. We learn as much as we can to be ready to help your world in a time of need. And that time will come.

There are few people that have been accepted to come in our world. We showed them the UFOs we build and the UFOs that come from other worlds located in strategic points in the universe. We let them use the machines that help us fly for short or long distances. We have imaginary elevators that we can access with the power of our minds. We communicate through our minds too. Extremely rare somebody is using words to communicate, we only speak with visitors when they arrive in our world."

"The gardens you have all around are so beautiful. The flowers smell so nice. The trees are absolutely breath taking. They glow in the light, like they are full of precious gems. I have never seen something like this in our world" Victor said.

"Yes, there are precious stones everywhere and they sparkle in the "*Great Light*". The "*Great Light*" gives life to everything and keeps us young, we never age."

"Are you all immortal?" Paul asked.

"Yes, we are."

"We heard three times today that the underworld people will come to the surface to protect our people when the time will come. How will you know when the right time is to come?" Victor asked.

"The Master of the World knows everything. He is the higher entity that watches the balance in between good and bad in your world. Meanwhile, many of us go to the surface at the time of crisis and bring the balance on the good side. When we go there, we are invisible. Nobody sees us. Nobody knows we are there. Sometimes people see that a miracle happened, when in fact it was us taking care of the human problems."

"Aden, will you come with us in the Red Realm, or you will stay home?" Victor asked.

"We will come with you, and we will come back home after. I cannot wait to tell my friends what marvellous this day is" Aden said.

A few monks approached Victor, his family, and friends. They have a few trays with gold cups and offered warm beverages to all. Everyone all took a cup and started to drink.

"The taste it incredible! It's like nothing I savoured before. It's delicious" Grigore said. "What drink is this?" he asked.

"It is an elixir that we all have every day. This is the holy water. It keeps us healthy and young" Chodrak said.

"Oh, thank you. Can we have more?" Grigore asked again.

"You can have as much as you want in this world" Chodrak answered. "You cannot take it outside of this realm. This is the secret elixir given to us by gods at the beginning of time."

"What are these platforms that are used by people?" Victor asked curiously. "How can they fly with them?"

"We use these small platforms to travel everywhere we want in all the hidden worlds underneath the surface of the planet Earth. We keep a constant contact with all underground civilizations."

"Can we fly your platforms and visit your realm?" Victor asked, eager to see everything. "We would be very happy if we could do that."

"Sure, we will all go around my world."

By the power of his mind, Chodrak brought platforms for all, and said:

"Please step on them and do not be afraid. They are safe and well balanced. You will not fall."

Everybody stepped on one platform and felt very safe, like they were standing on the clouds.

"Let's go" Chodrak said. "We are very pleased to show you all our world."

As they were smoothly flying higher and higher above the houses, they saw the city from high above. The magical land was shaped like an eight-petalled lotus flower. In a far distance, clear blue water of the ocean stretched endlessly. The Sun above was shining majestically. Mammoths and dinosaurs could be seen across the land. Large fields of grains were surrounding the holy city. Everybody was quiet. The words had no power to describe the wonders in this realm. When they got back to the gate, the platforms softly removed themselves in a thin air.

"Mom, what are those huge hairy animals with long and curved tusks?" Victor asked his mother.

"Chodrak, would you please tell us a few things about mammoths? I thought that they are extinct" Sanda asked.

"My pleasure, dear friends. Yes, these animals are extinct for more than ten thousand years. Global warming happened so fast at that time that vegetation disappeared, and mammoths starved to death. But some of them found the entrances to our world and we created the perfect habitat for them. They are happy here and live in harmony with the dinosaurs and other animals that are extinct in your world.

Mammoths could travel a distance equivalent to going around the world twice during their lifetime.

As you can see, they are very large animals. They weight about six to ten tons. They had a fur coat in two layers, which they needed for the cold weather. Mammoths were herbivores. They ate bushes, leaves, all edible vegetation that they found in their way. They probably ate about seven hundred pounds of leaves and grass every day."

"How long did they live?" Paul asked

"They lived in between 60 to 80 years" Chodrak said. "In our world, they have no age."

"What did they use the tusks for?" Victor asked. "They are huge."

"We presume that they cleared the snow when they were traveling for finding food."

"I hope you all enjoyed this trip" Khalifa said. "We must give thanks to Chodrak for his elaborate description of his world, and to all people in this realm for their kind welcome. It is time to go to the Red Realm, where you will learn to control and play with magic. There are some tricks that you will see, and you will believe is magic, but in fact they are just tricks. You will have a great time playing these tricks in front of your friends in your world. They will be excited.

In this magic world, you will learn and practice magic. You can think at anything you want, and the world you created in your mind will be your own world. And there is a surprise waiting for you. Antoine, the great wizard himself, will teach you magic."

"Antoine? Mom, who is Antoine?" Victor asked with excitement.

"I've met him before. He is one of Merlin's apprentices. We all will enjoy this realm very much" Sanda said. "We will learn so much from him."

"How old is he?" Victor asked again.

"He is immortal, my dear," said Sanda.

"Victor, my dear son, I am sorry, but I cannot stay any longer, I have to go home to my new family" Alex said. "Your stepbrother is an infant, and he needs me."

"Ok daddy, thank you for coming today."

"I would never miss your birthdays for anything in the world" Alex continued.

"Which world: ours or this one? Hahaha, just kidding. Bye, dad."

"Bye everybody" said Alex waving goodbye.

"Goodbye, Alex!" said everybody at the same time.

Victor had tears in his eyes, as his father walked towards the exit.

Nemo was there in an instant and accompanied Alex to the exit of the Magic World. Close to the exit door, Mr. Nemo looked at Alex and said:

"You must know that you were accepted here today, in our world, just because Victor held your hand when you came here. And you must know that you will never be accepted here again unless you will change your heart. You hurt Victor so much when you left him and his mother to chase your career. He was six!!

Here, only people with good heart are allowed. Your heart is not pure. You are selfish and you care only about yourself. You must know that Victor is a special child. Not only that he forgave you, but he still loves you with all his heart. Now off you go. We wish you to find peace with what you did." said Nemo touching Alex's chest with his soft paw. "Now feel the pain that Victor feels when you walk away from him" said Nemo closing the door behind Alex.

Alex felt a great pain in his heart. He had to sit on a rock to catch his breath.

He understood what he has done to his son, but it was too late to change. Tears started rolling down his cheeks. Regrets overwhelmed his mind and body. He stood there, alone, and cried.

RED REALM

"Great! His father finally left, not that he was a threat to me. I could bite him hard…hi, hi, hi. Oh, I was waiting for this moment for a thousand years. Finally, they are coming in my realm. I will trick them easily. Hi-hi-hi!! The whole world will hear about me. I will prove to everybody that I am the best. My mom told me that, and I will not disappoint her. Hi-hi-hi!! Khalifa, here I come!" whispered Shadow.

ANTOINE, THE GREAT SORCERER

Toto touched the ground with his powerful trident and in an instant, everybody appeared in a different world, the Red Realm, the realm of true magic.

It was very weird for all people to see that nothing was in order there. There were signs with the names of the streets or towns, all pointing in a chaotic direction. Some were upside down, some were facing the earth, and some were pointing the sky.

Some streets were above them, and some vertical on their sides. Few houses were upside down, perfectly balanced on their roofs. Wow, what a chaos!!

But in all this confusing view, there was standing very calmly an old man. He has long grey hair and beard. Very graciously, he is holding with much confidence a long wood stick. Long robe and a cloak were his outfit, no jewelleries. What everybody could see and amazed them, was the look in his eyes. His blue eyes showed so much serenity, kindness, and humility, like nothing bothered him in his life. His smile was gentle and beautiful.

"Is this Antoine, mom?" Victor asked.

"Yes, sweetheart. This is Antoine, the great sorcerer. He was one of Merlin's apprentices, my darling. He has Merlin's powers. Let's introduce ourselves," said Sanda.

"Greetings to you, Antoine. It is a great pleasure to meet you again. I am here with Victor, my son. It is his birthday today and as my gift for him, I brought him here, in this Magic World. I invited my sister Gabriella with her family, and I am sure you remember her. Here are our parents, our uncle and our cousin with her family, our darling nanny, our best friends with their children, and Victor's best friends from school" said Sanda showing them all graciously with her hand. "It is an honour to meet you here, dear Sir. Tomorrow is the birthday of my youngest nephew, and we wanted to keep the family tradition to spend the birthdays of our children together, like we did in the past. This makes us all very happy" Sanda continues.

"Greetings to all, my dear. I am happy to be here to celebrate Victor's and Lorand's birthdays with you all" said Antoine with humility in his voice.

"Sorry to ask, Antoine, but why everything here looks like a chaos? Nothing makes sense" Victor said.

"My dear, I was just cleaning and dusting before your arrival" said Antoine with a naughty look. "Just wait and you will see what I was doing. Unfortunately, I didn't have enough time to finish my job. I hope you will like it."

"Would you please introduce us to magic?" Victor asked very courageous. "We want to know everything you will teach us."

"This is a great honour for me, and I will do it gladly. But first, let us to welcome you in this realm."

Antoine raised his right index finger, rotate it gently and softly blew all over the environment.

Magically, everything around came to life. They all found themselves in a middle of an intersection, where the signs pointed in all directions, the streets were wide, and the houses started to move. All houses were wearing huge white chef hats and had long skinny hands with white gloves. They were holding gold trays with many different delicious foods.

Surprisingly, the houses had eyes inside windows, mouths instead of doors, and they started to talk inviting everybody to taste their offerings.

"See, Victor? This is for all of you" Antoine said. "Enjoy!"

"Please come and enjoy my fresh cookies" one house said. On its forehead was written Casa de Prajituri (Cookies House).

"Mom, look, is written in Romanian" Victor said very surprized.

"Look over there too" his mom said.

Casa de Placinte (Pies House) was offering hot pies, like Victor's mom and grandma used to make.

Casa de Torturi (Cakes House) was holding few cakes in its hands, and there were many tables with many delicious cakes.

"Why is it written in Romanian?" Victor asked Antoine

"Everybody here can read in their own language" Antoine said. "You read it in Romanian, others read in English, or Italian, depends on where they came from. I read in French...ha-ha-ha"

"How is this possible?" Victor asked. "Is this a trick?"

"No trick, it's magic," said Antoine.

"Let's eat" Andy said. "It is dinner time, right?"

"In our world, yes, it is dinner time" Gabriela said. "The time stays still in this world."

Casa de Torturi (Cakes House) had two huge cakes with lighted candles on top and said:

> "Victor and Lorand, come over here. Make a wish and blow the candles. Whatever you wish now and here, will come true in your world. This is magic too."

The boys closed their eyes, made a wish, and blew the candles, and everybody started to sing Happy Birthday. It was a happy moment. Sanda and Gabriela had tears in their eyes, and they hold each other handswith so much love, very proud of their children.

> "Let's ask Merlin to join us here today," said Antoine.

> "How can we do this? Is he available?" asked Victor.

> "We call out his name and he will be here" answered Antoine.

All people called his name "Merlin", and he was there.

> "Greetings to you all, my dear friends. I was wondering if you would like to meet me here today," said Merlin.

> "Merlin, I didn't know that you really exist. I always thought that you are a fruit of ancient people imagination" said Victor with surprise in his voice.

> "Of course, I exist. I am everywhere. I am omnipresent in your world and this one" said Merlin smiling.

Cakes House started to cut slices of cakes for everybody. Merlin moved his finger and a beautiful long table and chairs appeared in front of them. Cakes House placed gold plates with slices of cakes on the table in front of each and everyone.

And then, there was a surprise. The three houses started to dance and sing:

"Happy birthday to you
Happy birthday to you,
Happy birthday Victor and Lorand,
Happy birthday to you!"

"Mom, the houses are singing and dancing! That's magic, right?" Victor asked his mother.

"Yes, it's magic, my dear. This is Merlin doing just for you two" she said.

"Happy Birthday, Victor!" said Shadow with sinister smirk. *"You will never forget my gift to you. Hi-hi-hi!! Just wait and see"*

They all started to eat the delicious cakes, talking, and laughing happily.

"Merlin, are you immortal too?" Victor asked.

"Yes, I am, like everybody in this magic world. We all are immortals in this realm or in yours."

"What do you have to do to be immortal?" Victor asked.

"Live your life in such a way that everybody remembers you with love," Merlin said. "Do good for the humanity; love, be always kind, and help everybody without expecting anything in return. Everybody will keep you alive through their mind and heart."

"Will I be happy doing this?" Victor asks curiously.

"Nothing and nobody can give you more satisfaction than dedicating your life to others, and this will remain in the history forever" Merlin said.

"Who are you really, Merlin?" Victor asked.

"Oh, my dear, I am everything and everywhere. I am the priest of nature, and the keeper of knowledge, specially of the hidden secrets. I have a great wisdom and powers from the two opposing forces: good and evil. I have prophetic powers, I can see both past and future, I am eager to advise and be of service, but I am unable to change what I know must happen.

I was and I am the greatest sorcerer of all times, a prophet, a tutor, and I was the advisor to the great kings, including King Arthur… well, good times."

"Where have you been for such a long time? Nobody knows anything about you after the great adventures you had with King Arthur" Victor said.

"I've spent a millennium in the woods and during that time I was known as the Wild Man of the Woods. I learned how to control the nature, how to talk with animals, and how to enhance my spells in controlling the weather, and then I decided to do my magic in this perfect Magic Wonderland. Everything what you see here is magic and in the meantime it's very real."

"Please tell us something about your life that we do not know from the movies or books. My mom read to me books about your adventures, and I always wanted to be like you after enjoying the stories. How did you become a wizard?" Victor asked.

"Oh, my dear, I was born a wizard. My destiny was written before I was born. My mother was the Royal Princess of Dyfed who had become a nun. My father was an angel who visited my nun mother and left her with a child. People said that my father was an evil spirit who impregnated my mother during her sleep. Because of that, I was baptized very early in my life; they didn't want me to be evil like my father... but I couldn't be like him. I've never met him. My mom raised me with so much love. I could speak almost as soon as I was born. She taught me that. My mom was very special. Everybody loved her." said Merlin with nostalgia in his voice.

MAGIC TRICKS

"Let's start with some tricks that you can play with your friends. Shall we?" Merlin asked the children.

"Yes, yes, yes" said the children in unison.

"Ok, first I want to know who knows how to use a calculator."

"Me, me" said some of the children.

Merlin raised his finger, and in the blink of the eye, the children had calculators in their hands.

"Now, chose one number in between one and ten."

The children started to press the number on the calculators.

"Do you all have your number?" Merlin asked.

"Yes, yes" children said.

"Multiply the number by two," said Merlin.

The children did it.

"Now, multiply the number by five" Merlin continued.

"Done" children said.

"Now, I will tell you your number after you tell me your final number."

"Mine is one hundred" Victor said.

"You chose number ten."

"My final number is fifty" said Lorand.

"You chose number five."

"My final number was forty," said Paul.

"You chose number four."

"My number was ten" Andy said.

"You chose number one."

"I can't use a calculator yet, I am just a little girl, and I cannot learn this trick" Ioana said with tears in her eyes.

"Please stop crying" her brother Mihai told her. "You will go to school soon enough and I will teach you all the tricks that we learn here today."

"It is correct, Merlin, but how do you know this?" Victor asked.

"This is a trick, not magic" Merlin said. "It is easy. I just remove the zero number at the end of your final number, and I got the initial chosen number. Ha-ha-ha, this is so funny" Merlin said. "Do you want more tricks to know?"

"Oh, I get it. In fact, you multiply the number by ten, and you remove the zero from the final number" Victor said.

"It's easy, isn't it?" Merlin said. "Now, do you want new tricks?"

Yes, yes," said the children.

"We can play tricks with our friends at school" Paul said.

"And nobody will believe that Merlin taught us" Victor said. "Ha-ha-ha!!!!!"

"Do you know the magic trick in which you will know for sure the age of your parents?" Merlin continued with a big smile on his face.

"No, we don't know" children said.

"Give the calculators to you parents" Merlin said.

"Mom, dad, take the calculator" children said to their parents.

"Now is your turn, my lovely parents. Do not be shy about your age. You are at least a millennium younger than me" Merlin said. "Ha-ha-ha …!!!"

"Now, multiply your age by two, then add one to it. Multiply the number you got by five, and again multiply it by ten." Said Merlin.

"Sanda, what number did you get?" Merlin asked.

"3450. Am I that old?" Sanda asked laughing.

"No dear, you are 34 years old. Gabriela, which is your final number?" Merlin continued.

"3650, Merlin."

"You are 36 years old, my dear friend."

"Oh, I got it, Victor said. You removed the last two digits from the final number."

"Correct" Merlin said. "You are smart children, no wonder about it. I knew this, though."

KRITON AND THE MAGIC ARROWS

"Now, everybody will get a wand," said Merlin. "Your spells will come true as soon as you use it. But you must know that the magic is in your heart, not in the wand. The wand is only an instrument to help you focus your energy. Always be positive and visualise what you expect to happen and focus on the outcome. It is especially important to know that when you cast a spell, you must have calm emotions. You must always be in control. If you are upset about anything, it will influence the effect of your spell. Your spells must be clear and concise. If you are vague in what you want to happen, the spell can turn out in unexpecting ways. The most important thing to remember is that you must believe you have supernatural powers over natural forces."

"Did it happen to you to be affected by emotions?" Paul asked.

"Of course, my dear. Even if I was the greatest wizard in the world, I am still a human being and I still needed to learn, and practice being focused."

"Can we do magic outside of this world?" Paul asked.

"Yes, you can. Never forget that the magic is in your heart. When you honestly believe and use the right spell, your magic wish will come true."

"Mom, dad, I want to be a magician" Paul said. "Please!!"

"Of course, my dear. You can be if you want to" Gabriela said.

"I want to be a magician too," other children yelled with joy. "Me too, me too!"

The parents smiled at their children with love. The kids knew that their parents would approve and will always be there for them.

"I am sure you remember The Great Kriton. He came here to tell you how to make the magic arrows" Merlin said.

"Hello, hello, hello" Kriton said to everybody. "As I promised, I came here to let you know the art of making invincible arrows. But because you need sharp knives to make them, I will tell you only how they are made. We do not want you to get hurt today."

"Hello Kriton, we are so happy to see you here" Victor said. "Please tell us everything."

"Ok then. First, you need dry wood branch which is easy to bend. We always got the straightest sticks from dried trees. Each arrow should be about half as long as the bow, or as long as the bow can draw back. Smooth the surface as much as you can, for a better aim. When done, put the metal arrowhead on top. The right arrow sticks are straight and dry. With a sharp knife, make an arrow shaft on the opposite side of the arrow. Place the arrow shaft on the arrow rest of your bow. Now you are ready to draw the bow back. Keeping your bow arm steady, simply push your fingers on the bowstring out of the way of the string. The string will snap forward, and your arrow will start to fly. Aim the target and let the arrow hit it. I wanted to mention to you that the centaurs are the best in making arrows, bows, and in using them. They are very precise in aiming, never missed a target. And to make them invincible, Merlin will show you the magic spell required. He helped me all along to make them indestructible" Kriton continued.

"Now, I will tell you how to add magic with the arrows. As I told you, the magic is in your heart" Merlin said. "Raise your hands and you will get bows and arrows."

Merlin just moved his finger, and everybody got them.

"Before you aim the arrow, you can put a spell on it in your own words, or you can do it in your mind. Just make sure that the command is clear, short, and precise.

There are targets in front of you, and you can start shooting when you are ready. Do not be afraid, nothing can hurt you or anything around you. We will make sure of that."

Everybody shoots at the target, but Victor. Some hit it, some missed, but that didn't matter. The important part was knowing how to make the arrows and how to aim for the target.

Victor still didn't raise his bow and arrow.

"What happened, my dear?" Sanda asked her son.

"Mom, Merlin said that if we are upset about anything, it will influence the effect of our spell" Victor said.

"Are you upset, my dear?

"I am not upset; I am just thinking of my dad. I wish he was here" Victor said.

"My dearest friend, your father loves you very much, but he had to go" Khalifa said.

"Yes, I know that, but I just wish he was here to see me shooting my first arrow. He misses so many things I do, all the time."

"Do not worry my friend, we will show him when he will be allowed to come in this realm. He must change his heart before he will be accepted in here again" Khalifa continued. "Now just concentrate and aim the target. Do not forget the spell and believe that you have superpowers."

Victor raised the bow and the arrow, aimed the target, and gave an order to the arrow in his mind: *Do what I tell you to do. Hit the target.*

At the same time as Victor shoots his arrow, Merlin released a white dove in front of the target.

"*Save the dove*" Victor commanded to the arrow.

The arrow was invisible in an instant, passed through the target without leaving any marks on it. The dove flew away without being hurt.

"Why did you do that?" Victor asked Merlin.

"I wanted to see your confidence. I heard your commands. You have seen the danger, and you acted accordingly. Your main concern was to save the dove. This is what a true magician does: save the animals and save the people. You will be a great sorcerer one day, if this is what you want to become. And one more thing: the dove was made of paper" Merlin said.

"But it looked so real" Victor said. "I wouldn't hurt anybody. I believe now; this is what I will do in my life. I will protect people and animals."

"It looked real because I wanted it to look like this. This is magic too" Merlin said. "Your arrow went through the target but didn't leave a mark on it. You had the power to make the arrow invisible. This is very rare quality for a magician."

"I know you helped me with this" said Victor with humility in his voice.

"No, my friend, it was all you," said Merlin. "I will take you as my apprentice for the years to come."

"Years?" Victor asked very surprized.

"Yes, dear, for years. It requires hard work to become a great magician, and I know you will do great things in your life."

"Thank you, Merlin. I will be very happy. Mom, may I, please? Khalifa, will you be with me during the lessons?"

"Of course, nothing will stop me" Khalifa said. "Your mom will know that I will be in great hands, … ha-ha-ha…," Khalifa laughed.

"Of course, my darling. Khalifa will be here with you all the time. I would love to be part of the training too, if you will let me," said Sanda.

"Mom, I want you to be here with me. And we can tell daddy everything I've learned, right?" asked Victor excited to be Merlin's apprentice.

"Right, my darling. We will tell him everything," said his mom.

Sanda felt her heart breaking in millions of pieces. She felt her son's pain. She wanted to comfort him, but she knew that whatever she will do for her son, will not fill the void in her son's heart.

MAGIC PLAYGROUND

"Here is your playground" Merlin said. "Do as much magic as you want. Become invisible, change the water in elixir, transform your devoted pets in everything you want. I am sure they will not mind. Just use your imagination and be confident in your spells."

"They can change in other animals too, without our spell" Paul said.

"Not in this realm, my dear" Merlin said. "I blocked their powers and their magic. Here you are the only ones how can use magic, and me, of course."

"I don't want to transform Khalifa in any other animal. I love him so much. He is so fluffy and cute" Victor said.

"Ne neither, me neither" said the children pointing at their pets.

"That's fine, you don't have to. It was just an idea" Merlin said. "Do the magic you want to do."

Victor took his wand and pointed it at a water fountain that was close by. "*Water, make water fish, water sea horses and water mermaids*". The water started to make the fish jumping out of the water, sea horses laughing happy with the mermaids riding them. The water seemed to be dancing. "*Water, be ice, now*" said in his mind, still pointing the wand on the fountain. The water was frozen in an instant. "*Add sparkling and colourful gems*".

A wonderful, wonderful, unique water creation was unfolded before their eyes.

"Wow, it's so beautiful, my dear" said Sanda to her son. "It's amazing. How did you come up with this?"

"I wanted to paint in water like you paint on canvases" Victor said. "The difference is that I used magic, you use your heart."

"Oh honey, you used your heart too. Otherwise, you couldn't do this. This is a piece of art. I am so proud of you" Sanda said.

"Thank you, mom. What magic will you do?"

"I will paint this moment on a canvas. I want to paint all of us here, and I will make copies for everybody" Sanda said. "I want to save this moment in time".

A huge canvas, oils, an easel, and brushes appeared in front of her, when she used her wand.

"Paint them all" she ordered to the brushes and the oils.

The oils started to combine in wonderful colours, the brushes strokes gave life to the canvas. Everybody was painted in bright colours, and it show their spirit. They were all happy. When the painting was done, somebody was missing. *"Paint Victor's father beside him"* Sanda said.

In an instant, Alex was right there beside Victor, holding his shoulders, looking at him with so much love. *"Paint all our dear animals"*, Sanda ordered. Each pet was painted on the canvas beside their masters. Now the painting was finished. It was so beautiful. Each of Victor's friends and family was gifted a copy of the painting.

"Who wants to do the next magic?" Victor asked. "I can't wait to see what you can do."

"I will be invisible" Mickey said.

"No, you will not, my dear. Me and our children will stop your spell with our wand. Let's do something together" Gabriela said. "Let's fly."

"Yes, let's do it" her children said.

Holding their hands, they all started to fly up high, laughing and laughing, excited to continue with their adventure.

"I will be a centaur," said Zaya. "Kriton, can you take me in your world?"

"It will be a great honour" Kriton said.

Zaya used her wand and transform herself into a beautiful young woman centaur, and, in an instant, they disappeared in a different world.

"Grandma, grandpa, what you want to do?" Victor asked Nastasia and Grigore.

"We want to watch you only" said Victor's grandfather. "Just being with you here today is magical for us. We love you all so much, the words cannot describe how much. We love you forever, in this world and after we are gone. When you see the Big Dipper in the clear sky in the night, you will know that we will be sitting on it, watching over you. We will always be with you."

"We love you too, grandpa," said Victor.

"I want to make gold out of stones" said Tannis. "Merlin, is this possible?"

"Everything is possible, my dear. Just believe it" Merlin said. "Do you want me to help you?"

"Yes, please."

Merlin touched Tannis's wand with his magic finger. Tannis said: "*Be gold*" pointing a big rock on the side of the road. Like magic, the stone was a huge gold rock. It was so shiny, so beautiful.

"Too bad I cannot take it home" she said. "I would love to surprize my mom" said Tannis.

"The only gold your mom needs are you," said Merlin. "What you will do in your life will be gold too" Merlin continued.

"Thank you, Merlin. I will tell my mom what you said, if this's all right" Tannis said very excited.

"Of course, you can. There are no secrets here" said Merlin with a big smile on his face.

"I want Christmas" Aden said. "We do not celebrate Christmas in our world. May I?"

"I want Christmas too, me too" children said.

"That's a lovely idea. You must make snow, decorate the houses, make cookies for you and Santa" Merlin said.

"Yes, yes, we will do" said the kids being very excited for Christmas in September.

Mihai and Ioana put their wands together and said looking at the sky: "*Snow!*". Miraculously, it started to snow with huge flakes, but it was not cold at all. The temperature did not change.

"How is this possible?" Mihai asked Merlin.

"I thought I could help a little," said Merlin laughing naughtily.

"Yes, it is very helpful, thank you" answered Mihai.

"I want to make a snowman" said Ioana.

"Me too, me too," said other children.

Rada and Radu decorated the houses with a simple word pointing to them their wands: "*Lights*".

"Ha-ha-ha!!! The houses started to laugh. It's so ticklish … ha-ha-ha…"

"More lights!" Radu said, and more lights appeared on the housed and on the streets.

"Ha-ha-ha, we love it!" said the houses in unison.

Cookies House offered everybody fresh baked cookies on gold plates.

"We need milk! Santa loves cookies and milk," said Rada. She used her wand and glasses of milk were very nice displayed on the tables for everybody to take.

"We need carrots for the reindeers" said her brother Radu. He moved his wand saying: "*Carrots*", and lots of fresh carrots were ready for the reindeers.

Merlin looked at the excitement of all children and decided to surprize them. He moved his finger and jingles were heard in the realm. Santa was coming with his flying reindeers.

"Mom, look, Santa is here!" said Victor with excitement in his voice. "Christmas in September!"

"Wow" said Aden. "I cannot believe it. It's my first Christmas. I will tell everybody in Gold City, they will be so happy to hear that. We know about Christmas only from books or stories of the travelers. Santa, I was a good boy!" he said to Santa.

"Ho, ho, ho!! Merry September Christmas!!" said Santa approaching them all riding his sleigh with his reindeers. "I know you were a good boy" he said.

"Me too, me too," said the children.

"I know, I know, I wouldn't come if you were naughty. Ha-ha-ha… I will come in every December to your underworld, Aden, but you just must help me to get the approval to get there. I know that is very strict."

"I will do my best, Santa. All children will love you there," said Aden. "Their hearts are pure as crystal. There are no naughty children."

"I know that my dear. What do you wish for your first Christmas, Aden?"

"May I have a crystal globe with you flying on your magic sleigh led by your reindeer in the snow, please?"

"That's the perfect gift for you and for the children in your realm. Can you take them to your friends?"

"Thank you, Santa. I will do it. They will be so happy" Aden said fast, like he didn't want Santa to change his mind.

"Ho-ho-ho, here they are, my new friend. Now, all children come over here and you will get an early present for the year," said Santa.

"Will we not have gifts under our Christmas trees?" Victor asked. "I want my gift when I wake up in the morning, like all the children in the world."

"Of course, you will get gifts. The spirit of Christmas lives in the house of the believers, and I know you are a believer. You come from a long line of believers."

The children were so happy while they opened their gifts from Santa. Just seeing Santa, it was a gift itself.

Nichola started to play a Christmas song with his guitar. Somehow, the melody was different, softer, touching the harts of everybody there. This was magic. Everybody started to sing like a well-practised choir. They were all amazed when they finished the song.

"This was Merlin doing, right?" Sanda asked.

"Who else? Of course, it was Merlin. He makes this happen with his finger," said Gabriela.

"Ho-ho-ho, I must go now, my dear friends. My elves are waiting for me in my world. Tell all nonbeliever children that Santa is real and is watching. They must be good all year around to get gifts, or if they are naughty their stocking will be filled with coal.... ho-ho-ho...Merry September Christmas!!!"

Santa flew high up in the shy on his magic sleigh and his magic reindeers, back to the North Pole.

"Ho-ho-ho!!!" was heard across the realm as he disappeared into his magic world.

"Goodbye, Santa. Thank you for coming for us" Victor said.

"Ho-ho-ho!!!" was heard very softly, like in a dream.

"Mom, we saw Santa. Isn't this amazing? For sure all children will believe us. We will show them the presents we got from him."

"That's wonderful, my sweetie. You have to know that these gifts have magic in them. If you want to see Santa, just take it in your hands and he will be there. Let's try not to call him too often. He is very busy all year round," said his mom.

"We will be good children and we will not call him," said Victor. "Right, my friends?"

"Right, for sure" answered the children.

"Please children, learn how to be invisible. Please, please, please. I promise I will be invisible too. I will play your game." said Shadow hoping that he will be heard.

HOW TO BE INVISIBLE

In an instant, Mickey said again:

"Let's learn how to be invisible"

"Children, do you want to learn this? asked Antoine. We will show you how. It's easy, but you need to believe and use your wands"

"Yes, yes" said children at the same time.

"All right, then. Listen and follow precisely what I say. This magic might become dangerous if not applied correctly. You must always have the wand with you. Do not leave it behind. You will need it to come become visible again," said Antoine.

"Now, close your eyes and in the eye of your mind, start imagining yourself surrounded by a bright shining sphere. When you literally see it, imagine in your mind that the sphere stops being shiny and progressively gets darker and darker. Feel yourself melting into the lights of the sphere and become one with them.

Now start repeating to yourself. "*Light pass through and around me, nobody will see me. Light pass through and around me, nobody will see me* ". As you imagine yourself becoming invisible, be as quiet as possible. If you make a noise, we will know where you are. We will hear you. And one more thing. Do not forget to think about the place you want to disappear to. This place must be very clear in your mind and see yourself in your hiding place. Gently touch your body with your magic wand, and you will be invisible".

"*Yes, yes, tell them how to disappear, stupid children. I made this naughty plan to kidnap Victor while he will try this invisibility trick… yuck… and Khalifa will have no other choice but to give me his crown if he wants his friend back. Hi-hi-hi!*" laughed Shadow. "*I am so smart…hi-hi-hi…The whole world will know that I am the smartest King*"

"When you want to come back, touch your body again with the wand, and see the process in reverse. Imagine the dark sphere becoming brighter and brighter. Let yourself to be engulfed by the light, and you will be seen again." continued Antoine. "Do you want to try?"

"Yes, yes" said the children being very excited to be invisible.

"Who is the first one?" asked Antoine.

"Let me try, please" said Lorand. "I am not sure that I will have this chance tomorrow. There are so many places to visit in this realm and I want to see them all"

"Sure. Come here and do exactly what I said."

Lorand closed his eyes. Everybody could see his cute little face being focused on the steps to follow. He touched his body with his wand, and he vanished.

"Mom, mom, he did it," said Victor. "Can he see us now? We can't see him!"

"Yes, he can see us, and I am sure he is so happy now" said Sanda smiling at her son.

A tornado of lights appeared from nothing and Lorand was seen by everybody.

"Victor, it's amazing. I could hear and see everything and everybody. It was so fun to be hidden right beside you and nobody saw me…. ha-ha-ha. I loved it" said Lorand. "Thank you for letting me be the first. Now it's your turn."

Victor closed his eyes and started imagining the bright sphere. He saw the lights engulfing his body while they started to fade away. He touched his body with its wand and disappeared.

Everybody was waiting for Victor to reappear. They waited and waited, and they got concerned.

"Antoine, where is my son?" asked Sanda

"I do not know where he went. We can't know unless he speaks loudly, and we will hear him".

"Look. His wand is here," said Sanda.

"Hmm…something must have happened," said Khalifa. "I am sure he performed his spell correctly. His wand shouldn't be here…hmm."

WHO IS SHADOW?

"Mr. Khalifa, Mr. Khalifa" called Mr. Nemo running to him.

"Lilly, the Flower Fairy, told me that she has seen Shadow coming out of his shield. She said that he was right behind Victor when the poor child had his eyes closed saying the spell. Lilly saw Shadow pushing Victor when he touched his body with his wand, and he lost its wand. I believe they are both in the same place, and both invisible." said Mr. Nemo almost crying. "We must find Victor. I am afraid that Shadow will hurt him."

"Shadow, hmm? And today was the day to be released after a thousand years of punishment. How could I forget this? I was so happy to be here today with Victor and Shadow took advantage," said Khalifa. He was so sad; he hardly could breathe. "I failed my friend, and I was responsible for his safety."

"Mom, Khalifa, I am right here in front of you," said Victor.

"Is Shadow with you?" asked Khalifa.

"I don't know his name. It is a hyena, and he has big teeth. He keeps showing them to me," said Victor.

"Stop talking, you insignificant boy. They can't do anything to rescue you. You are trapped now in this invisible realm where I have the power. You mean nothing to me. One more word, and I will eat you, bone by bone! Shadow was speaking to Victor.

"Why are you doing this to me? What is it that you want?" Victor asked Shadow. "I did nothing wrong to you. I don't even know you. Please let me go to my mom. I am sure she is scared"

"Quiet! I told you to stop talking! I need to concentrate now." said Shadow with an angry voice.

There were a few moments of silence that felt like an eternity. Sanda was so scared indeed for her son's life.

"Antoine, Merlin, please do something. Please save my son!" begged them with tears in her eyes.

"We will when the time is right. Just trust us and Khalifa," said Merlin.

"Khalifa, my friend, do you remember why and how Shadow was trapped in a shield for a thousand years? I am sure this has something to do with what is happening now, but I do not remember. My memory is not that good now" asked Merlin.

"Yes, of course I remember. Me and Mr. Nemo found Shadow, who was a cub at that time, at the entrance in this realm. He was hungry, wet, and cold. We took him inside. We fed him, play with him, and tried to teach him our ancient wisdom."

"Liar, liar!" was heard Shadow screaming. *"You kidnapped me from my mom!"*

"No dear, we did not. We found you right here, lonely, and scared. You told us that your mom was killed by an antelope while she was hunting them for your food. We took you in, and treated you like one of our own. We even loved you" said Khalifa with a kind voice.

"Right, it's true," said Mr. Nemo. "We loved you"

"Liars! Nobody loved me, but my mom. She taught me how to hunt, how to laugh, how to be a leader of my clan. I was the prince of my world, but no, you had to come and "save" me...yuck. When there was the time to be the King of Small Animal's Realm, you took the crown. It was supposed to be mine. My mom told me that I will be King one day. You took this dream from me and from her. You, Khalifa, stupid cat, are my enemy and Victor is mine now, unless you give up on your crown and give it to me. Now!!!" said Shadow with authority.

"Victor, hyenas are predators, which means that their instinct is to chase anyone that runs away. Please stay calm and stay put and wave your arms. If Shadow comes forward towards you, take a few steps towards him. Do not be afraid. He will not attack you.

Shadow will feel threatened by you. Make yourself look aggressive, and Shadow will think that you will attack him, and he will run away," said Khalifa.

"This trick it's not working now. Here I have control. I am not afraid of a little boy. He makes me sick of how small and innocent is he. Khalifa, why did you change my name? My mom called me Bandit, which is a perfect name for me. But no, you had to change it. You called me Shadow. I am not a shadow, I am a ferocious hyena with the best education in chasing, hunting a prey and eat their flesh." said Shadow with so much hate in his voice.

"My dear, we called you Shadow because wherever we went, you followed us as a shadow. You were small and cute. You loved us too, or at least you showed us," said Khalifa.

"Love…yuck…what is love anyway? Do you really think that this word means something to me? Why did you punish me under the crystal shield for a thousand years?"

"My dear, love conquers all. To answer to your question, we wanted to give you time to see what animals in this realm do, how they love, protect, and serve all children. We hoped that you will see and learn. We hoped that your heart will be melted by the children's innocence, love, and laughter. It seems like you learned nothing. You are the same greedy and naughty little hyena" said Khalifa with so much sadness in his voice.

"Give me my crown and your precious friend will be released" commanded Shadow.

"My dear, a crown will not make you king. A true king is considerate, he has a big heart. He loves and protects his kingdom and his people, or animals. But come and take it. You will be responsible for everything happens in this realm and the one above. You will have to take decisions, every day" Khalifa said to Shadow.

"Put your crown down and I will remove the invisibility spell. I will have my crown and your friend will be free".

Khalifa put his crown on the ground and was waiting to see Victor free. They all were waiting, but nothing happened.

"I can't remove the spell. You took my magic" said Shadow to Khalifa.

"You never had magic, my friend," said Khalifa. "You thought you had. We gave you some magic just to feel one of us "said Khalifa.

Khalifa was standing there thinking how he can release his friend…and he remembered.

"Victor, do you remember when your mom sang you a lullaby when she put you to bed? Can you sing it?"

"Yes, I remember it" answered Victor.

"This lullaby always calmed you down. I want you to be calm and sing it, please. Just trust me" said Khalifa knowing what he was doing.

SANDA BOCA

Victor started to sing, and his mom accompanied him:

> "Somewhere over the rainbow
> Way up high
> And the dreams that you dreamed of
> Once in a lullaby
> Somewhere over the rainbow
> Blue birds fly
> And the dreams that you dreamed of
> Dreams really do come true
> Someday I'll wish upon a star
> Wake up where the clouds are far behind me
> Where trouble melts like lemon drops
> High above the chimney tops, that's where you'll find me
> Somewhere over the rainbow blue birds fly
> And the dream that you dare to, why, oh why can't I"

Victor saw Shadow closing his eyes, feeling very sleepy, and whispered:

> "He is falling asleep, mom"

> "Do not stop," said Khalifa. "Keep singing"

Victor continued singing watching Shadow at the same time:

> "Someday I'll wish upon a star,
> Wake up where the clouds are far behind me
> Where trouble melts like lemon drops
> High above the chimney top that's where you'll find me
> Oh, somewhere over the rainbow way up high
> And the dream that you dare to, why, oh why can't I?"

Everybody was waiting to see what will happen. Shadow was in a deep sleep. Victor looked at him and he couldn't believe it.

"He is just a cub" Victor was thinking. "He is so cute now"

In an instant, Victor became visible, the spell was removed. Shadow didn't have power anymore, he was asleep.

"Mom, I am here. Thank you, Khalifa." said Victor hugging his mom and his cat.

"I was not scared, and I knew you will save me"

"I am so happy to have you back" Khalifa told to Victor.

"Victor, we are so happy to have you here. We were so scared." said his friends.

"This is the way that we could trap him in the shield for a thousand years. We put him to sleep. Merlin, what can we do about Shadow? Can we change him in a mouse? asked Khalifa.

"No, please don't. He is just a cub, and he misses his mom, his brothers and sisters, and his friends. He doesn't want to be here. He wants to go back." said Victor protecting Shadow.

"And what do you want us to do?" asked Merlin.

"Take him back in his world, please," said Victor. "He will be happy there"

"We do not know where his family is. We had found him here at the doorsteps," said Khalifa.

"I know where his family is" the fire dragon Nyre said. "Sometimes I go out in their world just to watch and learn. I have seen his family looking for him. They were calling for him and were so sad because he was not found. I can take him tonight"

"Thank you, Nyre," said Khalifa. "You are a true friend"

Nyre took Shadow in his claws and flew away. Everybody knew that Shadow, or Bandit, will be all right. They knew that he loved his family more than any magic was given to him. They knew that he was just a little puppy who missed his mom and family, and they all wished him all the best.

"Let's thank Merlin and Antoine for being with us here today. We must go," said Khalifa. "But before we go home, I have something to do. Will you all come with me?"

"Yes, we will come with you."

"Thank you, Merlin!!! Thank you, Antoine!!! We will not forget what you taught us!!!" said the children waving goodbye.

"See you soon, my friends. Victor, I will wait for you to come back. I will make you my new apprentice. I haven't had one in a thousand years. I want you to have my powers and with Khalifa beside you, you will serve and protect all mankind."

"I will be back. Right, mom and Khalifa?" Victor asked his mother and his cat.

"That's for sure, my darling. Now let's see what Khalifa wants to do" said Sanda to her darling child.

WHO WILL BE THE NEW KING OF SMALL ANIMALS' REALM?

When Victor and his friends and family got to the exit door of the Magic World, Khalifa asked them politely to let him speak.

"Please, my friends, be patient with me. I must do something that I was waiting to do for a long time. As you know by now, my father was Zeus. I took this form, and I was waiting for a child to be gifted in wanting to learn everything about everything and to use magic like no one before. Today I am so proud to have Victor as my pupil. I will devote my life to him, teaching him everything I know, in fact everything that everybody in this magic realm knows.

I dedicated my life to many children, waiting for the right one. So here we are, and I am honoured to let you know that Victor is the one I was waiting for thousands and thousands of years."

"Bravo, bravo," said the people.

"It is a very hard decision for me that I must take now. Who do you think will take the responsibility to be the new King of Small Animal's Realm? There are so many great choices in this realm. They all are dedicated and willing to replace me. I need your help in deciding now. Will you help me?"

"Yes, yes, yes," said Victor and everybody else.

"I was thinking of Mr. Nemo, continued Khalifa. He is always here helping everybody, doing magic to change things for good, always smiling and his heart is as big and pure as mine."

"That's true" Victor and his mom said at the same time.

Everyone agreed.

"Ok, then. Mr. Nemo, would you do us the honour of join us now, if you can?" Khalifa said with loud voice that was carried all around the Magic Wonderland.

"Here I am, my friend, the honour is mine. How can I be at your service?" asked Mr. Nemo with a huge smile on his face.

"My dear friend, as of today, it is my honour to tell you that you will be the new King of Small Animals' Realm. Please take the crown as a symbol of dedication and loving heart of yours. We all believe that you will do great things and all animals will be taken care of."

"Oh, what an honor, my dear friend. I am gladly accepting the crown. My heart will always be open for all small animals or anybody else who will need my help. I swear!!!"

"We know and we will see you tomorrow," said Khalifa. "We have another gifted boy to celebrate his birthday tomorrow. The life that we knew it will be changed. New chapters will be written in our lives. We must go now. It is very late in our world and the children must go to sleep.

Farewell, my friend."

"Goodbye all, Mr. Nemo said. It was a great pleasure to be at your service today. Our doors will always be open for you. Tell all children about us, we will wait for you and all of them. When you come back, we will take you to different realms where you will learn how to control the earth elements: air, fire, and earth. The water realm revealed to yourself, and you know how to master the water. The fairies, ogres, giants, leprechauns, goblins, and other mythical creatures are eager to show you their magic worlds."

"Are there more realms in this Magic Wonderland?" Victor asked.

"It is a MAGIC Wonderland after all, and here everything is possible. As we said, if you believe, you will see" said the new King of Small Animals' Realm.

"See you soon, Mr. Nemo. Thank you for todays' journey in this magic wonderland," said Victor.

"Thank you, bye-bye," said everybody.

Mr. Nemo came close to Victor and whispered something to his ears. Victor looked at him and nodded his head. He liked what he heard, and said:

"I promise. We will do," said Victor.

Huge fireworks were all around the realm. The lights were so colourful and bright.

"Wow, it's so beautiful," Victor said.

"Yes, it is. Now it's time to say good night to everybody," said his mother.

"Thank you all for coming today" Victor said. "You made my day very special. Tomorrow we will celebrate your birthday, Lorand. I can't wait."

"Me too, Victor. Today was a glorious day. Mine will be the same" replied Lorand.

"Good night, good night, everybody," said his friends.

THIS IS NOT THE END

It's the middle of the night. It is a quiet night, with the stars dancing in the clear sky, and the Moon softly touching the Earth with its bright white light. Victor is sleeping in his bed with Khalifa beside him. The Moon light wakes him up.

"Khalifa, I had a wonderful dream. We went to a Magic Wonderland" Victor said yawning.

"Aha" said Khalifa with half open eyes.

"It was amazing. There were so many magical animals and I made lots of friend" Victor continued.

"Yes, you made many friends" Khalifa whispered.

"And you were talking. Hey, you are talking with me right now and I understand you. I must be dreaming! Mr. Nemo told me to ask my mom to write a book about this magic world. He said that in this way all children in the world will know about them and their parents will start to believe."

Victor was very excited, but still the night was young; he was so sleepy, but now he knew it was not a dream.

> "We will tell her in the morning, my dear friend. Now go back to sleep," Khalifa said. "A great adventure is waiting for you tomorrow. Sweet dreams, my friend."

> "Sweet dreams, Khalifa."

Victor and Khalifa fell asleep in an instant. Victor knew he will continue his dream or his reality about the Magic Wonderland.

He knew this is not the end of a great adventure. He knew in his heart that this is only the beginning.